When in Das Biergärten...

"It's kind of cool that there's all these trees in the middle of the square like this," Siena said, looking around. "I always wondered why they were called beer gardens, and now I get it."

"They're chestnuts," Chen said, "planted to shade the cellars that the brewers kept their barrels in years ago."

Siena gaped at her. "How do you know all this?"

"Chen read her entire Munich guidebook cover to cover...twice," Meg said.

Siena just shook her head in awe.

"I have to take a break from bio every once in a while." Chen shrugged.

"Hey, if you've got the gift, put it to good use. And now we won't have to pay for a guided tour." She took a swig from her beer mug, waiting for the tartness to make her cringe. But the beer actually tasted great between bites of sausage and potatoes—the flavors all blending. It was like the world's most perfect comfort food, or Germany's anyway. Siena raised her mug to her new friends.

"Here's to an amazing semester in München," she said, clinking her mug to theirs.

"And to *Biergärtens*," Chen said.

"And to breaking rules," Meg said, giggling and giving Siena a nudge.

Siena smiled. A day and a half ago, she'd left the only home she'd ever known. But as she laughed and talked in the shady grove of chestnut trees, she thought maybe she could find a second one here.

S.A.S.S.
STUDENTS ACROSS THE SEVEN SEAS

The Sound of Munich

Suzanne Nelson

speak

An Imprint of Penguin Group (USA) Inc.

SPEAK
Published by the Penguin Group
Penguin Group (USA) Inc.,
345 Hudson Street, New York, New York 10014, U.S.A.
Penguin Group (Canada), 90 Eglinton Avenue East, Suite 700, Toronto, Ontario, Canada M4P 2Y3
(a division of Pearson Penguin Canada Inc.)
Penguin Books Ltd, 80 Strand, London WC2R 0RL, England
Penguin Ireland, 25 St Stephen's Green, Dublin 2, Ireland
(a division of Penguin Books Ltd)
Penguin Group (Australia), 250 Camberwell Road, Camberwell, Victoria 3124, Australia
(a division of Pearson Australia Group Pty Ltd)
Penguin Books India Pvt Ltd, 11 Community Centre, Panchsheel Park,
New Delhi - 110 017, India
Penguin Group (NZ), Cnr Airborne and Rosedale Roads, Albany, Auckland 1310,
New Zealand (a division of Pearson New Zealand Ltd)
Penguin Books (South Africa) (Pty) Ltd, 24 Sturdee Avenue, Rosebank, Johannesburg 2196,
South Africa

Registered Offices: Penguin Books Ltd, 80 Strand, London WC2R 0RL, England

Published by Speak, an imprint of Penguin Group (USA) Inc., 2006

3 5 7 9 10 8 6 4

Copyright © Suzanne Nelson, 2006
All rights reserved
Interior art and design by Jeanine Henderson. Text set in Imago Book.

LIBRARY OF CONGRESS CATALOGING-IN-PUBLICATION DATA

Nelson, Suzanne Marie, 1976-
The sound of Munich / by Suzanne Nelson.
p.   cm.—(S.A.S.S.: Students Across the Seven Seas)
Summary: Siena Bernstein attends school in Munich for three months,
where she perfects her German language skills, flirts with her attractive resident advisor,
and attempts to find the man who helped her father's family escape East Berlin in 1962.
ISBN 978-0-14-240576-5 (pbk.)
[1. Study abroad—Fiction. 2. Schools—Fiction. 3. Interpersonal relations—Fiction. 4. Germany—
Fiction. 5. Berlin Wall, Berlin, Germany, 1961–1989—Fiction.]
I. Title. II. Series.
PZ7.N43765Sou 2006
[Fic]—dc22 2005051609

Printed in the United States of America

For my parents, in thanks for the countless family vacations that first introduced me to travel adventures. And for Chad, who met me in Austria when no one else could.

The Sound of Munich

Glockenspiel (detail)

Theresienwiese

Siena's Munich

Universität München

Englischer Garten

Residenz

New Town Hall

Marienplatz

Old Town Hall

Hofbräuhaus

Sendlinger Straße

Viktualienmarkt

Name: Siena Bernstein
Age: 17
High School: Ocean Vista High
Hometown: Santa Barbara, California
Preferred Study Abroad Destination: Munich, Germany

1. Why are you interested in traveling abroad next year?

Answer: I want to explore my family's German heritage and learn more about the history and culture of my ancestors.

(Truth: It's my destiny to find the man who changed the course of my dad's life. And it's a nice perk that I'll get to cross state and international borders for the first time, too!)

2. How will studying abroad further develop your talents and interests?

Answer: I've always wanted to learn to speak German to keep my family's legacy alive, and this is the perfect opportunity.

(Truth: I want to answer the eternal question: What is up with lederhosen? I'm all for freedom of expression, but come on! Please tell me my great-grandfather never actually wore those things!)

3. Describe your extracurricular activities.

Answer: Member of the Ocean Vista Yoga Club, Barrista at Sweet Sara's Café, Astrology Columnist for Ocean Vista High Herald

(Truth: I start every morning with an aura-lifting chai latte from Sweet Sara's and my daily horoscope. Hey, until I know what the stars have to say, how can I do anything else?)

4. Is there anything else you feel we should know about you?

Answer: I am a driven, hard-working individual who will be a wonderful asset to the program.

(Truth: Karma, people, Karma! This trip was fated. That's all you need to know.)

Chapter One

Siena Bernstein knew the second she opened her eyes and saw daylight streaking into her room that something was horribly wrong. Why wasn't it still dark outside? She sat up, grabbed her itinerary off her nightstand, and squinted at it through half-open eyes.

"Oh my God," she gasped, and leaped out of bed, tripping over the sleeping bag on the floor. "Get up, Lizzie! Now!" She tugged on her jeans, then nudged the motionless mound in the sleeping bag with her foot. A muffled groan rose from its depths, followed by a shock of rumpled red hair.

"Siena, if you're waking me up for any reason other than

an earthquake or an Ashton Kutcher sighting, you're going to have to find a new best friend," Lizzie said, pulling a pillow over her head.

Siena gave the sleeping bag a yank while trying desperately to tie her favorite orange-and-pink batik scarf around her waist. "Seriously, I am in full crisis mode right now. We overslept. My plane leaves in three hours. It'll take us two just to get to the airport."

That did the trick, and Lizzie was throwing on her clothes in a matter of seconds. "I knew we should've set an alarm. Your mom never remembers to wake us up." She glanced at her watch. "We'll make it. You're just going to have to let me drive to the airport."

Siena ran a brush through her jet-black hair, ignoring the few stragglers that refused to lie flat against her head. "This from the girl who's gotten three speeding tickets in less than six months?" She snorted. "Good luck convincing my mom."

Lizzie glared at her. "Do you or do you not want to get to Germany before the school semester starts?"

Siena grinned. "Yes, I want to get to Germany."

"Then I drive," Lizzie said triumphantly.

"Fine." Siena grabbed her shoes and raced to the bedroom door. "I've got to go downstairs and get my mom." Then she froze as her eyes fell on her empty suitcase. She had packed and unpacked at least five times since yesterday afternoon, and finally, at two in the morning, decided to sleep on it before trying again. This had not been a wise decision. "Oh, crap. I could've at least picked which underwear to bring. Now what?"

"We decided spontaneous packing was more 'Zen,' remember? Your words, not mine." Lizzie shrugged. "At the time it seemed like a good idea."

Siena sighed. There was no way she could put together a whole semester's wardrobe in fifteen minutes. "How—" she started, looking over the piles of discarded clothes all over the floor.

"I'll pack," Lizzie said. "You go get your mom and say good-bye to Foster. The poor guy's probably down there crying into the cappuccino machine right now."

Siena hesitated. This was the story of her life. Whenever she needed to plan ahead, her brain flat-out rebelled. It was one thing for her to agonize over which of her clothes to bring to Munich for three months, it was another thing entirely to agonize over what outfits Lizzie would pack for her. Siena was all about bohemian panache—tunics and sarongs were her domain. Lizzie, on the other hand, was halters and extra-low-rise jeans. The possibilities were frightening. But if she didn't get moving, she wouldn't make it to international soil at all.

Siena shrugged and headed for the door. "Don't forget to pack my good-luck tee."

Lizzie pulled a BUDDHA IS MY OM BOY shirt from the pile on the floor. "Would I ever?"

"And *don't* pack anything that screams 'American tourist,'" she yelled over her shoulder.

"I'll try not to be insulted by that," Lizzie called back.

Siena ran down the back stairs to her family's café, leaving Lizzie to the haphazard packing. As she stepped through the back door of Sweet Sara's, she breathed in the warm smell of brewing coffee and fresh-baked muffins. Sometimes the ocean breeze carried the scent up the stairs to the second-floor apartment where she and her mom lived. She'd miss that smell over the next few months, along with all the other things about the café that she loved. The worn books that lined shelves along the back of the space, free for browsing. The knight in rusty armor—dubbed Moe—suspended above the coffee bar. The red London phone booth in the corner that she and her mom were especially proud of salvaging from the local junkyard (although they still wondered how it had gotten there in the first place).

Her dad and mom had opened Sweet Sara's in Santa Barbara right after they got married. Her dad had even named it after her mom. It was one of the last things he had done before he died in the car crash—one of the last things they had to remember him by. Actually, Siena only had pictures to remember him by, since she'd been three months old when he died. But the café had the same warm feel that Siena always imagined her dad having, too. That's why she and her mom could never let it go.

Last year, it had been touch and go keeping it running. Money had been so tight, Siena hadn't even wanted to tell her mom about the S.A.S.S. study-abroad program. She'd applied, but figured she had zilch chance of ever getting in. After all, she was the girl who'd had a blue ribbon at the fifth-grade science fair awarded to her project by mistake, the prize later given to that Einstein wannabe Jimmy Frou instead. (She and her mom had put all of her homemade aromatherapy oils to great use, though, even if those "unenlightened patriarchal judges," as her mom had called them, didn't appreciate the antibacterial effectiveness of tea tree oil.)

She'd always done pretty well in school (science fairs excluded), but that was only because of Foster's torture—er, tutor sessions. Foster was the rules guy, making sure Siena kept her head on straight, in class at least. She still couldn't quite believe there hadn't been some mistake with her S.A.S.S. application. Considering her past academic luck, she figured the Big One would sink California before she ever got to leave it. But then, shocker, she'd been accepted...with a scholarship! And now she was going.

Siena stepped into Sweet Sara's kitchen, where she found Foster pouring organic whole-grain muffin batter into baking pans. Foster had been Siena's next-door

neighbor since the two were toddlers. He was the closest thing to a brother she'd ever had, and he always knew how to make her smile.

"Hard at work, I see," she said to him, then grimaced at the huge tub of batter. She was usually the baker, complete with hairnet and neck-to-toe apron. At least Foster could get away with wearing a baseball cap with his short hair. The hairnet was the number one reason Siena hadn't had a date in six months. It gave off a bad vibe, any way you looked at it. Baking was one thing about Sweet Sara's that she wouldn't miss at all.

"I thought you'd forgotten about me," Foster said, "slaving away making muffins and soy lattes." He glanced at his watch. "You're late."

"What else is new?" Siena grabbed three warm muffins and put them in a bag along with a cup of coffee for the road.

"Don't look at me," he said. "I told Sara to wake you up over an hour ago."

"How many reminders did you give her?"

"None."

"Well, there's your problem. She needs at least one a minute." Siena grinned. "And I'd never leave without saying good-bye to you, my best friend, second only to Lizzie, who is, at this moment, performing unspeakable crimes of fashion to my luggage." She rolled her eyes. "So are you going to live up to your end of the bargain while I'm gone?"

She was always trying to get Foster to ask girls out more often. Or ask them out period, for that matter. This year, she'd made him swear that if she made it to Germany, he'd ask a girl to spring formal. She could tell from his hesitation now that this was not a likely possibility.

"I refuse to give in to peer pressure," he finally said.

"That's why you have us to help you," Lizzie said as she walked in lugging Siena's two suitcases behind her. "And I heard what you said about my packing, Senni. You doubt me now, but you'll thank me later when you've got European guys begging for your number."

"And who says I need any help in that department?" She shook the bangles on her arms and struck a belly-dancing pose. "It's only a temporary dry spell I've been going through."

Siena laughed at Lizzie's defensive scowl. "Thank you for packing for me." Then she turned to Foster. "And thank you for helping Mom out with Sara's while I'm gone." She gave him a big hug. "Make sure Moe's dressed for any special events, okay?" It was Siena's job to dress up the knight for all major holidays, and over the years his costumes had gotten pretty creative.

"No prob," Foster said. "Just bring me back a beer stein."

"Foss, a beer stein is all wrong for you," Lizzie said. "What you really need is some lederhosen to wow the ladies."

"Lederhosen might be even more disastrous to a love life than a hairnet," Siena said.

Lizzie laughed. "After a semester of my tutoring, Foster will be able to flirt in anything, even lederhosen."

"Just the thought terrifies me," Foster said.

"Come on, Lizzie," Siena said, heading toward the dining room. "I've got to get my mom."

"Hey, Senni," Foster said. "I hope you find what you're looking for over there."

"Me, too," Siena whispered.

Only Foster and Lizzie knew the reason why Siena had been dying to get to Germany. She'd never told her mom the whole truth, because her mom never talked much about her dad anymore, and Siena was starting to feel like the whole topic was a little taboo. Besides, this was something Siena needed to do on her own—something she'd wanted to do for years. If things worked out like she planned, by the time she got back from her semester abroad, she'd be able to tell her mom everything. If not, then she never had to tell her at all.

She and Lizzie found her mom behind the coffee bar, whipping up some frothy chai lattes.

"Morning, chickadees," Sara said. "All packed and ready to go?"

"You're slacking off in the maternal department, Mom." Siena laughed. "You were supposed to wake us up two hours ago."

Her mom glanced down at her watch. "I forgot! I can't believe it! I'm so sorry." She pulled her apron off and dug under the counter, searching for her keys.

"I've got 'em!" Lizzie cried, triumphantly dangling the car keys from her fingertips. "They were in the sink. Let's go. I'll pull the car around."

"Nice try, Lizzie," Sara said, "but I've seen your manic driving before. Hand them over."

Siena laughed as Lizzie, defeated, reluctantly gave up the keys. "Are you sure you can leave the café for a while?" she asked her mom.

Sara smiled. "Are you kidding? Foster can do the job of three people. He was here at four this morning, starting the coffee before I even came downstairs." She laughed, then headed for the door. "You girls grab the bags while I get the car."

Outside, the early-morning sunlight glittered on the ocean. It was going to be another seventy-five-degree, sunshiny springlike day—the kind most out-of-towners envied. But Siena had always thought that a little snow every now and then wouldn't be so bad. For that matter, a little bit of any kind of change now and then wouldn't be so bad. The Pacific Ocean was beautiful, and so was Santa Barbara. But she needed a change. She jumped as a car horn blew behind her.

Sara stuck her head out of the driver's-side window and motioned for Siena and Lizzie to get in.

Siena had just closed the car trunk when she remembered. "The Carpe Diem List!" she whispered to Lizzie. "It was on my desk last night!"

"You didn't put it into your backpack?" Lizzie rolled her eyes. "Like mother, like daughter."

"What's the holdup?" Sara asked.

"I'll be right back, Mom," Siena yelled as she raced up the stairs to the apartment. There it was, sitting on her desk where she'd left it. She folded it, careful not to tear the crisp, old paper, and slipped the list into her backpack. As she climbed into the car, she made a silent wish for it to bring her the good karma she'd need if she was going to go through with all of her plans for the trip.

Siena had always known that her mom and Lizzie shared a psycho-driver streak, but her mom set new records on the way to the airport. LAX was the closest major airport to Santa Barbara, but it was no picnic to get to, especially in commuter traffic. Luckily, they got there with forty-five minutes to spare, but then Siena had to stand in a huge line to check her two bags.

By the time she got to the security screening gate, the voice over the intercom was already announcing her plane's boarding.

"You'll make it," her mom assured her. "But this is as far as we can go."

"Don't go getting empty-nesty once I'm gone, Mom. I

get wind that you've started wearing a bra or some other horrific midlifey thing, and I'll be on the first plane home. Got it?"

"Me? Wear a bra?" Her mom laughed. "Please."

"Don't worry your little cosmic head," Lizzie said to Siena. "Foss and I will keep her social life hopping."

"Lizzie, like I said before," Sara said, "you can't keep up with me."

Siena smiled. Not only would this trip be the first time she'd ever been out of the state of California in her life, but it would be the first long trip she'd ever taken without her mom. The two of them had only had each other to rely on for so long, sometimes it felt as if they were more sisters than mother and daughter. Siena would miss their early-morning cappuccinos, their thrift-store shopping sprees, their late-night gab sessions—everything about their duo.

"I'll call whenever I can," Siena said.

"Don't you dare. You'll give me a bad reputation," her mom said. "I don't want anyone to mistake me for an over-protective PTA mom." She visibly shuddered at the thought. "You just have fun and let yourself go. You've worked so hard for this scholarship. Now enjoy it, will ya?"

Siena hugged her mom. "I'll miss you."

"You, too, sweetie," Sara said.

"What about me?" Lizzie asked. "Where's the love?"

"I'll miss you, too," Siena said, throwing her arms melo-dramatically around her best friend.

The intercom announced the final call for her flight.

"Now go before your plane leaves without you," her mom said, giving her a playful shove toward the security gate.

Siena smiled as she ran toward her gate with her heart racing. This was it. She was saying good-bye to everything she'd ever known. Sure, she'd dreamed about this for years. But now she was living it.

Siena pressed her forehead against the airplane window to get a better view. Thousands of feet below, the peaks of the snow-crested Bavarian Alps were breaking through the scattered clouds. They went on as far as she could see, jagged, immense, and beautiful. She felt a rush of adrenaline. Not only had she left California less than twenty-four hours ago, but now she had left America, too, and was flying alone over a foreign country six thousand miles away from home!

She'd always wanted to see the world, as many countries as she could fit in, and now she was finally going to get that first stamp on her passport. It was the start of a whole new era—one chock-full of European flair, and maybe even a foreign fling or two. A small part of her did still wish she could be starting the spring semester of her junior year with Lizzie and Foster. But maybe, by this time next year, she'd have a hottie from overseas to bring to her senior prom.

She yawned and stretched, wishing she'd gotten more sleep on the flight from New York to Munich. But at least her flight had gone pretty smoothly, aside from the rough start getting to the airport.

By the time she had gotten to New York from L.A. for her connecting flight to Munich, she was exhausted. Six hours of flying with another eight to go (on a red-eye to boot) was not an exciting prospect. As she squeezed her way through the aisle, all she could think about was getting to her seat and passing out. She didn't see the girl's foot sticking out in the aisle until it was too late.

"Ouch!" the girl had shrieked as Siena stepped on her foot and half tumbled into the girl's seat. She looked close to Siena's age, but that was where any similarity between them ended. She was from-a-bottle blond and lanky, with carefully manicured nails and perfectly painted and pouted lips. Even though Siena was leggy, too (something she'd inherited from her dad), everything else about this girl was a complete contrast to Siena's minimal au naturel makeup and low-maintenance hair.

"You could have broken my toe," the girl had snipped.

"I'm so sorry," Siena cried, untangling herself from the seat. "Are you okay?" She tried to mask a giggle in a cough. Okay, she seriously needed to work on not laughing in situations like this, but it *was* kind of funny.

"Unbelievable," the girl muttered to the person seated next to her, intentionally loud enough for Siena to hear.

Siena had apologized one more time—it really had been an accident—then made her way to her seat a row behind. She sneaked another look at the blond girl as she stowed her backpack. She'd already opened her *Glamour*, her supposed broken toe forgotten. For the next three hours of the flight, Siena had watched as the girl, who she came to find out was Miss Briana Seabrook, pushed the flight-attendant call button a total of five times. Her shrink-wrapped chicken penne meal was cold, *she* was cold, her movie headset was giving her a migraine. Every time Siena was just about to doze off, she'd hear the flight attendant approaching. "Yes, Miss Seabrook, how can I help you?"

Siena had silently sent out a plea to the cosmos that whoever her roommate was in Munich, she was not anything like this Briana. She was just the type of girl Siena and her eclectic group of friends at Ocean Vista High couldn't stand—a "foxymoron," all looks, no substance. She'd finally fallen asleep for a few minutes just as the plane was flying into the sunrise over Europe. And now it was already Friday morning. Where had the night gone? She guessed this weird time-warp feeling was jet lag, and she hoped her dorm room had a nice fat pillow with her name on it.

"Guten Morgen mein Damen und Herren!" The voice came over the plane's loudspeaker, making Siena jump. She took a deep breath. Okay, she could do this. She'd taken beginning German back home. The "good morning"

part she had down, and she thought there was something about "ladies and gentlemen" in there, too. But now the flight attendant was talking so fast it was impossible for Siena to keep up. The loudspeaker went silent for a minute and then started up again in English, and Siena sighed with relief. If she couldn't even understand a simple "We'll be landing shortly" spiel, she would be up *Scheisse* creek trying to communicate in Munich. Even though her dad and her dad's parents had all come from Germany, she didn't have a clue when it came to the German language. Shouldn't something like this come a little more naturally to her? True, she hadn't ever known her grandparents, since they died before she was born, and her mom could not speak a word of German. But here she was, half-German for crying out loud, and obviously a disgrace to her heritage.

Of course, that was what this trip was all about, wasn't it? Uncovering her German side, wherever it was hiding. And this trip was for her dad, too. She reached into her backpack and pulled out the Carpe Diem List. Running her fingers over her dad's handwriting, she wondered, like she always did, where he'd been and what he'd been doing when he wrote this list.

She had found the Carpe Diem List in the box of his things that her mom kept under her bed. Her mom had shown her the box when she was ten, telling her that whenever she wondered about her dad, all she had to do

was look in the box to find memories of him. Siena had gone through the box over and over again. Aside from the home videos her mom and dad had taken right after they got married, the little mementos in the box were Siena's only connection to him. The Carpe Diem List, especially, was what she cherished. She smoothed out its corners and read through it one more time.

Bill Bernstein's Carpe Diem List

1. *Find my soul mate.* 1/14/84
   (This was the day her parents met.)

2. *Experience great joy.* 11/29/89
   (The day she'd been born.)

3. *Experience great sadness.* 10/13/85
   (The day her dad's father had passed away.)

4. *Eat jellied eels, cow tongue, and Rocky Mountain oysters.* 10/20/80
   (That one almost always made her gag.)

5. *Go skinny-dipping at midnight in the Mediterranean Sea.* 2/15/89
   (Nine months before Siena had been born...heh-heh.)

6. *Fly around the world at least once, although not necessarily all at the same time. 3/15/79 and 6/8/85*

7. *Hike through the Grand Canyon. 6/10/78*

8. *Go skydiving. 4/12/87*

9. *Sing naked in the rain. 12/31/77*
(This sounded strange, but interesting, to her. And could be very cold!)

10. *Find Peter Schwalm and thank him.*

Only number ten was missing a date, and that was why Siena was on her way to Germany.

Her mom had told her the story of how her father had come to America. He'd been born in Berlin in 1959, and after the Berlin Wall went up in 1961, his parents started to plan an escape. "Your grandparents wanted to raise your dad in a free land," her mom had told her. "As soon as they were out of East Berlin, they planned to take your dad to America. But crossing into the west wasn't easy. Your grandpa George had a good friend, Peter Schwalm, who agreed to help them. He sewed a makeshift Soviet-army uniform in order to pass through the border unnoticed. In 1963, he hid your grandma and grandpa and Bill

in the trunk of his car. He built a smaller gas tank for the car so they'd all fit. They hid for hours in the trunk while Peter drove them far into the west. Then he took them to a friend's house where they could get passage to America.

"Peter went back to East Berlin to try to help more people escape," her mom had finished the story. "Grandpa George was never able to contact him after that. His letters from America may never have reached Peter. Your grandpa never heard from him again."

Each time she heard it, the story gave Siena chills. She pictured her dad, only four years old, huddled in that dark trunk, and her grandpa and grandma, risking everything to be free. But Siena had always hated that Peter Schwalm never knew they'd reached America safely.

Her dad, too, must have hated not knowing what had happened to Peter. After Grandpa and Grandma passed away, she guessed that her dad had wanted to see if he could find Peter. The Bernsteins owed him so much—their lives, their freedom. That must have been why he'd added Peter Schwalm to his Carpe Diem List. But her dad died only months after the Berlin Wall came down. Now it was up to her to find him.

What if the Peter Schwalm she was looking for didn't even live in Germany anymore? Or worse, what if he wasn't even *alive* anymore? She tried not to think about that. She'd come up with some ideas for finding him once she was settled in Munich. She'd do what she could, for her dad's sake.

She carefully put the list away and slid her backpack under her seat to get ready for landing. If her dad could take on jellied eels (she didn't even want to know what that involved) and skydiving, the least she could do was give his native language a legitimate try and get in touch with her German roots. Her mom had always told her she'd inherited some of her dad's spirit, and now was her chance to prove it.

The baggage claim area buzzed with people hugging, laughing, and chatting in a clucking combination of English and German. Siena's ears perked at each word of broken English, but even so, she noticed that most everyone at the luggage carousel spoke fluent German, except her. She scanned the bags rolling past. Her bags would be impossible to miss. Back at the L.A. airport, Lizzie'd had the brilliant idea of wrapping Siena's luggage in cellophane. Rolls of it were at the baggage check to secure fragile packages.

"Senni," Lizzie had said, "do you really want to fly your clothes halfway around the world without giving them some extra padding? Bad things happen when luggage rips open midflight."

Siena had laughed at the time, watching Lizzie wrap the

plastic around the two bags. Now she wondered what they'd both been thinking. She struggled to lift the cellophane mass off the carousel, then turned back to wait for her second, larger bag. But as the minutes passed, the baggage claim slowly emptied out, and there was no sign of her other suitcase.

A knot grew in her stomach as she looked at her one and only bag—its contents a complete mystery. For all she knew, Lizzie could've packed this one entirely with socks. She'd have to find the lost-baggage counter. But picking up this bag was impossible, especially since she didn't have anything sharp to cut through the plastic. She made a mental note never, ever to let Lizzie anywhere near her luggage again, and started half rolling, half kicking her bag away from the carousel.

"Guten Tag," a voice said behind her. *"Kann ich Ihnen helfen?"*

Siena looked up at a very tall, very cute guy with the bluest eyes she'd ever seen. And of course, she had chosen this very second to look like a total idiot, falling all over the bag at her feet.

"Um, *sprekinsy Deutch*?" she stuttered. "Er, no, I mean, English? *Spurrconzy Ingles?*" She cringed. What language was she speaking? Some warped mesh of pig Latin and Spanish?

She watched the corners of his mouth twitch. Oh God, he was either going to break into hysterical laughter or emit a slew of German expletives. Who wouldn't, after hearing his native language butchered by a foreigner? She was relieved when he smiled.

"Can I help you, fräulein?" he asked. His English held a hint of an accent, and Siena wondered how such a little accent could sound so sexy.

"I'm having a little trouble with my luggage," she said.

"There's luggage inside *that*?" He smiled, pulling out a ring of keys. "Let me see what I can do." He slid a key under the edge of the plastic cocoon and soon Siena's bag emerged from the layers.

"Thank you so much." She smiled into those aqua eyes. In Germany less than an hour and she'd already met a hot European. If things kept up at this rate, she was going to have a killer spring.

"I'm Stefan, by the way," he said, reaching out a hand to her.

"Siena," she said.

"Siena Bernstein?" Stefan asked.

"How'd you—" she started.

"Either I'm psychic," he said, his eyes twinkling, "or I have inside information."

"I'm hoping you're psychic," Siena said. "Then you can tell me where my missing bag is."

Stefan laughed and pointed to a name tag on his shirt that Siena hadn't noticed before. "I'm with the Foreign Cultural Immersion Program. I go to university in Munich,

but I'll be working as your resident adviser for the semester. I came to pick you up. Dr. Goldstein told me that you came to us through a S.A.S.S. scholarship, yes?"

Siena nodded.

"You're our only scholarship student this year. The other students better watch out. You'll be setting the curve."

"Did you hear my sad attempt at German before?" Siena laughed. "Not a chance."

Was he flirting with her? She couldn't wait to spill this to Lizzie as soon as she set up e-mail. She'd die.

Just then, she heard a high-pitched voice behind her that made her shudder.

"Stefan, how much longer will we have to wait? I'm exhausted."

Siena turned to see Briana Seabrook, surrounded by five huge suitcases (all in matching fabric, of course) and looking every bit the unhappy prima donna. It just wasn't possible that this girl was in her program. The gods of adolescence couldn't be that cruel, could they?

"Briana, this is Siena," Stefan said, "another student in the Intercultural Program."

Yes, they could.

Briana broke into a cool smile. "We met on the plane. Nice to see you again, Shawna."

"It's Siena, and nice to meet you, too."

Stefan turned to Siena. "Let's see if we can fill out a lost-luggage claim for your bag," he said. Then he gave

Briana a smile. "Why don't you wait here for a few minutes? Then I'll drive you both to the dormitory."

Whatever was in that smile worked like a charm. Briana visibly turned off her bad attitude and switched into full flirt mode. "Sure, Stefan. No problem. Is there someplace I can get some food while I wait? I haven't eaten since I left Manhattan. I wouldn't touch the airplane food."

Siena knew that all too well.

"I'm afraid there's only a pretzel stand here." Stefan pulled a pack of gum from his pocket and held it out to Siena. "This might help until we reach the dorm."

Briana took a piece, but when Stefan offered it to Siena, she shook her head. "No thanks. I'm a purist. The preservatives in that stay in your body for decades."

"Really?" Stefan's mouth half curled like he was trying not to smile. "I've never heard that before."

Behind her, Briana gave a short snort of laughter. "Safe-sex gum. That's a new one." At Siena's quizzical look, she added, not a little condescendingly, "*Preservative* means 'condom' in German."

Siena burst out laughing. Yet another one of those times when all she could do in a completely mortifying situation was laugh. She *really* needed to work on that. "See, Stefan, I warned you about me and German. The two of us are off to a rocky start."

"Not to worry. You'll learn quickly. But I may never think of gum the same way again." He grinned and picked up

Siena's bag. "Now let's go see about your luggage, yes?"

Siena followed Stefan to a luggage counter, where they got into a long line.

"This is going to take a while," she said apologetically.

"Don't worry," Stefan said. "Dr. Goldstein scheduled the program orientation for much later this afternoon. She likes punctuality, but we'll be there."

"I try never to rush anywhere. Life is long. There's lots of time."

"Is that a rule you always follow?" Stefan asked.

"Yes, and it gets me in all sorts of trouble, especially at school."

She laughed, and Stefan did, too. But then Siena looked over her shoulder at Briana, who was dabbing on lip gloss, no doubt in preparation for flirting with Stefan. She sighed. So far, she was missing half her luggage and the only person she'd met in her program was a total princess. Were the stars over this corner of the globe stacked against her?

Stefan must have seen a look of worry on her face, because he whispered, "Don't worry. Briana's not your roommate."

Siena smiled. "Stefan, you really *are* psychic."

Even if she was going to have to deal with a few snarky poseurs like Briana, it was nice to have some friendly (not to mention cute!) company in Stefan. Now if she could just figure out how to speak the language and find her missing suitcase, she'd be home free.

Chapter Two

Siena hadn't thought it was possible to get completely sick of someone in less than an hour. She was used to giving people the benefit of the doubt, especially since, face it, everyone had a few moments of bitchiness every once in a while. But after the car ride with Briana, she decided this girl's "moments" were pretty much constant. Siena tried to enjoy the ride, even with half of Briana's luggage sitting in her lap (there hadn't been room for all of it in the trunk and the front seat).

"Are you all right back there?" Stefan had asked, glancing back at her.

"We're perfect, thanks," Briana answered before Siena had a chance to.

Siena made a vain attempt to shift some of the luggage off her lap, looking out the window as the industrial airport area gradually turned into downtown Munich with its bustling streets and architecturally eclectic buildings.

She wasn't getting to see much of the countryside, but maybe that would come later, on some of the program's sightseeing trips. She'd always had a funky Brothers Grimm vision of this part of Germany, complete with Cinderella-esque castles and cottages nestled deep in the Black Forest. Of course, in the real Grimms' version of the story, one of the stepsisters cut off her toe to make Cinderella's slipper fit—not exactly a Disney happy ending. That's what happened to girls who fought over the same guy. And no guy was worth amputation, even if his eyes were the color of the clear blue sky.

"Everything is a mix of old and new," Stefan explained when Siena commented on the odd scattering of modern buildings and Gothic-style churches with their spires and bell towers. "Much of Munich was leveled during World War Two. Some of it was rebuilt to look like it did originally, hundreds of years ago. In the Marienplatz, the center of town, we even have a New Town Hall and an Old Town Hall. You'll see the plaza later. It's in a pedestrian-only zone, so we can't drive through it."

Out the window, she saw people wandering in and out of stores along the road. Awnings were up and the morning sun was shining down. She kept her eye out for the older buildings—the type dripping in history that she'd always seen in photos. They were beautiful, but being this close to them made them seem more alien to her, too. Was this the type of world her dad had been born into? She couldn't picture him here, but then again, she couldn't really picture him anywhere outside Sweet Sara's.

She was happy to see that the city was full of shops, cafés, and beer halls. It looked like it was easy to get around on foot. She'd definitely have to check out the social scene ASAP. There was probably already an e-mail from Lizzie waiting for her, pestering her for the lowdown.

"I'll bet you know a lot of great clubs, Stefan," Briana cooed from the backseat. "I've heard P1 is fab."

Stefan swiveled in the driver's seat, his face suddenly animated. "It's next to impossible to get into. I made it past the bouncers last year with some friends once. We heard DJ Prektik."

"Awesome," she said, turning on her smile. Then she glanced at Siena. "I'm sure you've heard of him?"

Siena shrugged. Of course she'd never heard of DJ whatever-his-name-was, and didn't care, for that matter. But it was just too easy to play along at this game. She couldn't resist.

"Nope," she told Briana nonchalantly. "I'm more of a HotSpot girl myself. You know, the L.A. club?" She and Foster and Lizzie had managed to get into HotSpot once, and had danced the night away. But just because she'd only been there one time didn't mean she couldn't make it *sound* like she was a regular. She continued, "Orlando Bloom and his buds like to hang there. I'm sure you've heard of it?" She threw Briana a sweet, unassuming smile that was met by steely silence.

Siena sat back, satisfied, but not before she caught a glimpse of Stefan's little half smile in the rearview mirror.

But Briana wouldn't give up that easily. She bent partway over Stefan's seat, leaning toward him. "My dad said he could get me VIP passes to P1 whenever, if you're interested. He works for the embassy back home."

"Thanks for the offer," Stefan said, his neck turning slightly red. "I'll let you know."

Siena shut her eyes for a minute, willing Briana to be quiet. The girl had apparently already picked her favorite boy toy, and Siena was just going to have to suck it up until the car stopped. Which, thankfully, it did a few minutes later, on a quiet little cobblestone street across from the university.

"Here's the FCIP *Schulheim*, or dorm. It's called Lebenhaus—the living house—more often, though." Stefan opened the car door. "Now I'll show you to your rooms.

You can freshen up and meet your roommates, then join everyone in the lounge on the first floor for orientation."

Siena grabbed her bag and squeezed out from under Briana's luggage. Stepping out of the car, she breathed in deeply. There was a little dampness in the air, and it was cold enough to feel like winter, but she guessed that made sense, since it was only the beginning of February. She was so used to California's warmth that this would take a little time to adjust to. There were no palm trees or bougainvillea lining these streets, and no tract homes with stucco walls, either. The old buildings surrounding the dorm felt as foreign to her as this country's language. It was all beautiful, yes. But she'd somehow expected to feel a stronger connection to it. She smiled and shook off the momentary doubt. She had three months to explore—three months to figure out how, in this country of her father's, she might belong.

When Siena opened the door to her third-floor dorm room, the last thing she expected to see was a five-foot, ninety-pound girl carefully straightening a paisley-and-floral-print comforter. She scanned the room, taking in a mound of lacy throw pillows and a row of tea-light candles. Well, she guessed every world needed some Martha Stewart style just to balance things out. A heart-shaped frame on the girl's desk held a picture of a crew-cut jock in a football

uniform, and a stack of CDs next to it looked frighteningly like country music.

"Siena!" the girl cried when she saw her, like they'd known each other for years. She rushed over to grab Siena's bag. "I'm so glad you're finally here! I'm Meg Young."

"Nice to meet you, Meg." Siena had never seen someone so small with such thick, long hair. Brunette waves fell down to Meg's waist, nearly hiding her petite frame. Meg ushered her into the room with an eager-to-please smile, and Siena couldn't help grinning herself.

"They told me your flight was getting in this morning. I got here yesterday, but I've been waiting to decorate until you got here. Except for this." She pointed to the comforter. "My parents sent it to me." She shrugged. "I guess they wanted it to feel like home."

Siena kicked off her shoes and stretched out on her bed. "Where's home?" she asked.

"Caldwell, Texas," Meg said with pride. "My dad's a rancher."

"Cool," Siena said. "I should definitely get something to cozy up my bed, too. It was nice of your parents to send you a comforter."

Meg nodded, then blushed as she looked at her bedspread. "I do kind of wish I'd gotten to pick it out myself, though. I guess it's pretty and all—" She stopped, then suddenly flopped down on her bed and sighed. "That's a lie. I hate it." She paused, then looked at Siena. "What do you think? Be totally honest."

"And you'll get nothing less from a Sagittarius," Siena said, looking at the comforter again. "As long as it suits *your* psyche, it's all good. Right?"

"But that's just it! The whole flowery thing is so...*Little House on the Prairie.*"

Siena shrugged. "The *Little House* motif works for lots of people. I'm down with Laura Ingalls Wilder. She was a feminist in real life, you know."

"But it's my mom's style...not mine. She has this whole color scheme for our house, so every room matches. She picks out everything."

"Wow, that's totally different from my place," Siena said. "My mom and I decorate together, and sometimes we make it a point not to match things. You know, just to spice it up."

Meg's face lit up. "Now *that* sounds cool. Can we try that? Maybe then no one will even notice my comforter!"

"We can definitely do something fab in here." Siena smiled at Meg. "Can we rearrange a few things? To unblock the flow of positive chi in the room."

"The what?" Meg asked.

"Oh, it's feng shui," Siena said, pulling her bed toward the center of the room. "My friends back in California are

totally into it. Do you know you can actually take a feng shui tour of Munich? I read about it on the net. How funny is that?"

Siena struggled with the bed for a few more seconds until Meg said, "Here, let me help. Where are we putting it?"

"It can't face the door or the windows," Siena said. "Can we put the two beds up against the other wall?"

"That would look so much better!" Meg said with a smile.

They moved one bed, and then the other, pushing the headboards against the wall.

"Hey, we could move the nightstands and dresser, too," Meg said.

"Now you're feeling the chi." Siena nodded. "What's your sign, anyway?"

"My sign?" Meg repeated.

"Astrological."

"Um...Aries, I think?"

Siena grinned. "I thought so! You're an adventurer at heart. You're all about change." She stood back to survey their work. The beds were closer together, with the dresser in between. The whole room felt less empty and more cozy now. "Not bad," she said.

"I love it!" Meg said. "Now we just need some decor that isn't so *Little House*."

"Could we go shopping after orientation this afternoon?" Siena asked. "Maybe get some strands of beads or something. Tranquil colors work the best—blues and greens."

Meg nodded enthusiastically at Siena's suggestion. "Sendlinger Strasse seems like the street where all the shopping is around here, within a reasonable price range anyway. I saw this vintage place yesterday that had some great scarves and pillows in the window. Maybe we can go there."

"Sounds great," Siena said. She thought fleetingly about how good an afternoon catnap sounded, but there was no way she was going to sleep away her first day here.

"Maybe we can even get Chen to join us," Meg said, nodding toward the bathroom. "If she'll leave her room, that is."

"Chen?" Siena asked.

"She's in the room next to us. We're sharing the adjoining bathroom. She hasn't come out much. She's from Boston. She ordered her textbooks in advance, and she's read all of them already."

"The weekend before the semester starts and she's spending it reading? I've got to hand it to her, at least she'll be well prepared," Siena said. "But she might also secretly be crying out for some spiritual release." Seeing the blank look on Meg's face, she clarified, "A.k.a. corruption."

"I don't know," Meg said, chewing on her fingernail.

"She seems nice, but she's kind of tough to get to know. You'll see what I mean." She eyed Siena's bag on the floor. "Wow, and I thought I was a light packer. That's pretty impressive."

"Not really. There's another bag where this came from. The airline just hasn't found it yet."

"I'd die if that happened to me," Meg said, shuddering.

Siena guessed Meg had probably packed everything in neat little rows, maybe even organized it all by color.

Siena shrugged. "It's not bad karma unless I'm missing my favorite T-shirt. Anything else is an easy fix."

She ignored Meg's look of doubt as she unzipped the bag to see what wonderful surprises Lizzie had packed for her. "Well, I've got underwear at least. But not much else." She laughed, staring at the meager contents of her bag— underwear, a couple of pairs of shoes and socks, and her toiletries. "I've been wearing these clothes since six A.M. yesterday morning. Who knows when I'll get the rest of my stuff? I'll just have to keep rewashing these, I guess."

Meg opened the closet doors and began rummaging. "Well, you're taller than me, but I might have something you can wear in the meantime."

Siena peeked into the closet at Meg's clothes. Definitely not a bohemian type—more like Banana Republic cardigan and capris. But the thought of wearing rumpled, sleep-worn (and possibly even smelly?) travel clothes to orientation made Siena cringe.

"Try on the pink pin-striped capris first," Meg said, loading Siena's arms with clothes. "Those are my favorite."

Siena smiled, but permitted herself one tiny sigh as she thought wistfully of her good-luck tee, flying high somewhere in the atmosphere.

A lavender sweater set and khakis weren't exactly what Siena had in mind when she'd agreed to borrow some of Meg's clothes, but after trying on the rest of the options Meg gave her, she knew it could've been worse. She'd at least managed to spice it up with a lime green scarf Meg had pulled out of the closet that she said her mom had made her pack. Siena had tied the scarf around her waist as a makeshift belt—it was a little too Eddie Bauer for her taste, but she could make do. Besides, she couldn't offend Meg by turning down a borrowed outfit. The girl was just too eager to help, and Siena was grateful for clean clothes, regardless.

When they walked into the student lounge, Siena scanned the room and spotted Stefan standing toward the back talking with a group of slightly older-looking guys and girls wearing name tags. They were probably the rest of the resident advisers. She hoped he'd look her way, but he seemed absorbed in the conversation, so she just enjoyed the view of his lean bod for a minute. On the other side of the room, she saw Briana and a few other girls who she could only assume were Briana's roommate and new

groupies, all leaning their heads together in full gossip stance. Briana looked over at Stefan and giggled, and the rest of her clique followed suit. Siena rolled her eyes. At least they could try for some subtlety.

She followed Meg to seats next to a beautiful, almond-eyed girl who was casually flipping through a biology textbook. Her hair was up in a French twist held in place by two pens, and her black blazer with satin cami underneath perfected the sexy-schoolgirl look. There was something about her that made Siena think of a slightly nicer version of Lucy Liu.

"Hi, Chen," Meg said, a little too enthusiastically. "This is Siena, my roommate! Isn't it great? Now y'all are both here. How fun!"

Meg shifted into hyperdrive chattiness as Chen raised her eyes from her book with a small smile. Siena had learned from Meg that Chen was planning on becoming a doctor. Her dad and mom were both surgeons—neuro and plastic. It was no wonder she had her biology book in tow—they were probably already pushing her for early admission to Harvard, poor girl.

"Hi," Chen said.

"How's it going?" Siena asked, plopping down in a chair and glancing at Chen's biology book. She caught a quick glimpse of a slip of paper with writing on it lying in the middle of the textbook, right before Chen snapped it shut.

"You do *look* like the perfect roomies," Chen said, nodding toward Siena and Meg's sweater sets. "Two peas in a knitted pod."

"Oh, these are Meg's." Siena laughed. "I'm missing some luggage. We're hitting a couple of stores this afternoon after orientation to see if I can find a few clothes to tide me over until mine appear."

"Why don't you come with us?" Meg chimed in. "We can go check out the Marienplatz afterward. I really want to see the Glockenspiel."

"Thanks for the invite. I'd like to, but I should study," Chen said, nodding toward her textbook. But Siena had a feeling that what Chen really wanted was to spend some time alone with whatever was written on that piece of paper in her book.

"Maybe Chen's right," Meg said to Siena, nibbling on a nail. "It's not a bad idea to get a jump start on our reading. From what I've heard about the Gymnasium school here, we'll need to study."

"Gymnasium?" Siena repeated.

"It's Germany's version of college prep," Chen explained. "Take AP classes, make them twice as hard, and you've got the Gymnasium. It's how brains like Einstein were educated."

"It's supposed to be tons harder than American high school," Meg said, worry lines creasing her forehead.

"All the more reason for me to get my shopping done before classes start, then," Siena said.

"You really should have one outfit that fits for the first day of class." Meg giggled, pointing to the too-short khakis Siena had on.

Even Chen gave a short laugh as she inspected Siena's obviously misfit pants. "Those give a whole new meaning to the term *high waters.*"

Siena laughed.

"Are you sure you don't want to come along, Chen?" Meg smiled at her. "You could help pick out something perfect for Siena, and it'd be so much fun if we could all get to know one another better."

A glimmer of a genuine smile sparked in Chen's face. She might have a tough-girl exterior, but inside, Siena guessed, her softer side was crying for release. It was just a matter of time.

"We do have a whole weekend of freedom ahead of us before school starts," Siena said. "Besides, someday when I'm all pruny and old, I don't want to remember my semester abroad as an ode to *Gray's Anatomy.*"

That tiniest hint of a smile on Chen's face was growing. "You sound like a walking, talking tourist promo."

"I just don't want to waste one second." Siena grinned. "This afternoon, I'm going exploring. But it's no biggie if you don't want to come. Maybe we can meet up with you later tonight on Sendlinger Strasse, if you change your mind."

"Hey," Chen said suddenly, "you're going to Sendlinger Strasse?"

"Yup. That's where you said all the cool stores are, right, Meg?"

Meg nodded. "I didn't go into any of them yesterday, but there were some awesome discount designer-clothing stores. You'll definitely be able to find clothes."

Chen's eyes brightened. "I'll go," she said. "But I'm bringing my biology book with me."

Siena gave Meg a victory grin. She wasn't sure what the magic words had been, but she was glad Chen had agreed to come along.

"She's a fire spirit," she whispered to Meg. "I can tell. She'll be trading her biology book for a beer stein in no time."

Good thing Chen agreed to the shopping spree before orientation started, because once Dr. Goldstein, the director of the program, began her overview of the semester, even Siena got nervous about the class structure. The Gymnasium was an intense advanced-preparatory program that got high-schoolers ready to attend universities. Since German universities had a limited number of spaces for new students each year, their standards were very high.

As the three girls compared their class schedules, they realized that this semester was going to be crazy tough.

European history, science, math, and German-literature courses were all required. There were no fluff classes—no painting, no culinary arts, no music or dancing, either. There was a film class, though, and although Siena had never held a camcorder in her life, she'd jumped at the chance to sign up for it when she put together her schedule months ago at home. She was hoping it might be an easy A.

"If I have any chance of keeping my scholarship, I'm going to need a science tutor," Siena groaned.

"You're on scholarship?" Chen asked. "Then you shouldn't need any help."

"Au contraire," Siena said. "It was only thanks to my friend Foster at home that I managed to pull off the grades for the scholarship. He's my Merlin. When left to my own devices, me and school mix like essential oils and water. Meg told me you're going premed in college, though. Maybe you'd consider tutoring me?"

"I'm not sure you want that. That last time I tutored someone, it didn't go so well," Chen said.

"Why not?" Siena asked.

Chen shrugged. "One minute I was explaining the Fibonacci sequence and monotone convergence, and the next, the poor kid was in tears. I think maybe some of the calculus was a little bit over his head. But it's all really so simple."

"Hearing a word like *Fibonacci*, whatever it is, would

have made me cry, too," Siena said. "But since we're not studying calculus here, I think I'll take my chances with you."

"All right," Chen said, trying to look stern while hiding a pleased smile. "But don't say I didn't warn you."

"Our job is not to babysit you," Dr. Goldstein was saying to the room of students, "but to challenge and enlighten you. Many of you may have taken advanced classes in your schools back home. But even those who have, may not have experienced a rigorous curriculum like ours." Her stern eyes stopped on each student's face, as if trying to measure the dedication and determination in each one of them. She looked the part of a tough German prof, too, with her salt-and-pepper hair swept up into a tight twist, her wire-frame glasses, and her black suit impeccably tailored and pressed. Siena was surprised when she suddenly smiled. "Now for the fun part. You'll be taking a number of organized trips to surrounding sights like Dachau concentration camp, Neuschwanstein Castle, and Salzburg, Austria. There will also be a three-day excursion to Berlin at the end of the semester. We don't encourage you to take trips by yourself or with friends during the program, but to participate in the planned group outings instead. But that being said, in Munich, feel free to explore as much as you like. Classes begin on Monday. You've got today and the rest of the weekend to get your bearings."

Siena's heart started pounding when she heard mention of Berlin. She'd actually get to see the place where her

dad and grandparents had crossed over from communism into freedom. If Peter Schwalm was still alive, maybe he'd stayed in Berlin all these years. She made a mental note to check the Internet later.

"We have a cafeteria that you're welcome to use," Dr. Goldstein continued, "but also take the opportunity to enjoy the culinary offerings of our wonderful city. And, if anyone's interested, I happen to know the best place to get apple strudel in all of München."

A few students up front laughed politely at that, and Siena noticed that Briana was among them. She had chosen a seat in the front row and was taking copious notes, hanging on every word Dr. Goldstein said. Why anyone would spend so much energy faking interest, Siena would never understand.

Dr. Goldstein introduced all of the resident advisers after that. "Their jobs are twofold," she explained. "They supervise the Lebenhaus, but they also act as tour guides for you during the program's activities and trips."

There was one RA assigned to each floor in the dorm. Since all the floors were co-ed, the RAs seemed to be a pretty even mix of guys and girls, and they were all students at the Universität München. As Stefan walked up from the back of the room to be introduced, he caught Siena's eye and gave her a nod. Siena smiled broadly at him, and then blushed when she saw Meg grinning at her afterward.

"We had a little vibe going on back at the airport this morning," she whispered to Meg as Dr. Goldstein kept talking.

"He is yummy in a Heath Ledger sort of way," Meg said.

Siena laughed. "So you noticed, too?"

Meg nodded. "But he's not my type. And I've got my boyfriend, Cody, back home. He's more the outdoorsy kind."

"I saw his picture on your desk," Siena said. "A football player, huh?"

"He's the varsity quarterback," Meg said proudly, blushing. She glanced at Stefan, and then back at Siena. "Y'all would look really cute together," she said. "Too bad he's off-limits."

Siena's heart instantly dropped. "He has a girlfriend?" she guessed.

"I don't know, but it's still a lost cause. Resident advisers aren't allowed to 'fraternize' with the students."

"Well, you know what they say about rules made to be broken." She winked at Meg.

"You wouldn't!" Meg said, looking slightly alarmed, but then breaking into a shy giggle.

"We haven't even started the semester yet and you're plotting subversive activities," Chen said. "Impressive. Stupid, but impressive."

"Hey, I might have more than one life to live, but that doesn't mean I'm going to waste a second in any of them,"

Siena said. "This will be a semester of firsts for me. First time abroad, first time in Germany, and if I'm lucky, first foreign fling." She grinned at Chen. "What about you? You could find the guy of your dreams here, too."

Chen laughed. "Not likely. Guys find me intimidating, don't ask me why."

"There are plenty of guys out there who love smart women," Siena said.

"It's true," Meg said with encouragement. "Napoleon and Josephine. Anthony and Cleopatra."

"Cleopatra killed herself," Chen said drily.

"Hey, at least she found true love first," Meg said.

Chen smiled and rolled her eyes good-naturedly at Meg's optimism. Siena had to laugh at her two newfound friends. A cynical brainiac and a sweet small-town girl— what a combination. She fell somewhere in between the two of them, and even though she'd only known them for a little while, it seemed like a perfect fit.

As Dr. Goldstein finished, the girls stood up to leave. When Siena looked for Stefan again, she saw that he was cornered by Briana and her clique. He was smiling and laughing, looking like he was enjoying every minute of the attention.

"It looks like somebody else is already working on breaking that rule," Chen said, nodding toward Briana.

"It doesn't matter," Siena said. "I don't do catfights, and besides, I don't even really know him."

Meg watched Briana for a few seconds more before grimacing. "Girls like that get me all fired up. She's like this girl from my school who always talks down to everyone around her. What's the point of being so snotty?"

"Let's get going," Siena said. "That girl is a drain to my aura."

Three hours later, with arms full of bags from their low-budget shopathon on Sendlinger Strasse, Siena stood in the middle of Marienplatz, the huge town square at the center of Munich's pedestrian zone. The edges of the square were lined with breweries, cafés, and the two town halls, old and new.

Siena set her bags down at her feet. During their shopping, she'd bought one outfit to wear while she waited for her luggage, a wind chime and some colored strands of beads for their room, and a henna tattoo kit that she was planning on testing as soon as possible on anyone willing (Meg and Chen weren't...yet). Meg bought some funky old advertising posters—in German, of course!—plus two Tibetan throw pillows for their dorm room. Siena was impressed; they were a far cry from the floral-print motif she'd started with. Chen, surprise surprise, bought herself a notebook for class. But Siena couldn't criticize, especially since it turned out that Chen was fluent in German, French, Chinese, and English. She'd already saved Siena from having to sputter cryptic German. At least Siena had

noticed that Chen opened her textbook only once or twice, and it was to scribble something down quickly. What was she writing in there anyway, formulas?

Siena had also made a great discovery over the course of their shopping spree. Chen had a closet addiction—shoes. Sure, the girl might be an out-and-out genius, but she was a genius with fantastic fashion sense. So Chen's notebook purchase was balanced out by the pair of discounted Prada flats she'd bought, too.

"Way to maintain the yin yang, Chen," Siena had told her afterward.

Now the three girls stood in the square, waiting for the Glockenspiel to give its five-o'clock performance from the clock tower.

"The Glockenspiel has forty-three bells that play four different tunes," Chen said, reading aloud from her Munich guidebook. "It portrays scenes from a royal Bavarian wedding."

"How neat!" Meg's eyes lit up. "I can't wait to hear it!"

Siena's eyes roamed over the clock's lacy details, taking in the beauty of it. A small crowd of people had gathered around, too, all waiting for the show. Just then, the clock struck five, and colorful figures emerged from the two archways toward the top of the tower. A bride and groom at a banquet table celebrated in one archway while a group of dancers spun around in the other.

"Those are the coopers." Chen pointed to the dancers.

"They were the first people out in the streets after the Black Plague passed, dancing to let others know it was safe to come out of their homes."

"If they were the first ones out, how did they know it was safe?" Meg asked.

"They probably didn't," Siena said. "But they still danced. That's what's so cool. It's the life force at work."

"Or insanity," Chen said.

Siena laughed as knights jousted in a tournament for the royal wedding and the coopers did their jig. When the last bells died away, the Marienplatz became a busy square again.

"We should get back to the dorm," Meg said. "I want to e-mail Cody before it gets too late."

"Can we go grab some dinner in the caf first?" Chen said. "It's been hours since we bought those pretzels at Sendlinger Strasse."

"It's still early in Texas, so I guess I can e-mail him later," Meg said. "And I *am* starving."

"Me, too," Siena said. "I have an idea." She grabbed the guidebook from Chen and stared at the map for a second. "Follow me," she said, and started off down the street with Meg and Chen hurrying to keep up.

The Viktualienmarkt was only a few minutes' walk from Marienplatz. Once Siena found it, she was immediately glad they'd come here. It was a great outdoor marketplace,

full of early-evening shoppers bustling from one stall to another to get fresh ingredients for their dinners. A huge maypole stood in the center of the market, and jutting out from it were colorful wooden plaques painted with Munich's beer barrels, brewmasters, and folk dancers. The stalls were full of merchants selling everything from fresh flowers to dried herbs and spice wreaths, and a tangy sweetness filled the air. After buying some fresh fruit and cheese to bring back to the dorm, the girls made their way to one of the beer gardens in the market.

Siena pointed to a kiosk where servers waited to dish up plates of steaming sausages, sauerkraut, and potatoes. Just looking at the food made her mouth water.

"This is dinner," she said with a flourish.

"It smells delish," Meg said. "Like something my mom would make back home."

"My mom would flip her vegan veggieburgers if she saw all this meat," Siena said, looking over the piping-hot trays. All of the sausages seemed different, and she had no idea which one she would like. She wanted to give some of her German skills another try, since she'd failed miserably with them so far. She waved to one of the servers.

"Was für wurst haben Sie?" she said. She thought that she'd managed to say something about sausage flavors, maybe. That was a start.

The server pointed to each tray of sausage. "Bratwurst, saure Zipfel, Nurnberger, und Schlachtplatte."

"Okay." Siena nodded. She could do this. *"Ich nehme sic,"* she said with finality, pointing at the bratwurst, and began digging through her purse for her euros.

"You must be very hungry," Chen said.

"I'm starved. Why?"

"You just said you'd take one of everything." Chen laughed.

"Oh no." Siena looked up to see her plate piled high with four different kinds of sausage. Thankfully, Chen stepped in and explained everything to the server, who chuckled and then replaced most of the food, leaving one bratwurst and adding some potatoes and kraut. *"Guten Appetit!"* she said, handing the plate to Siena.

"You just became my German tutor, too," Siena said to Chen.

"All right, but if you add one more class, I'll have to charge a fee," Chen kidded.

They made their way down the line to where beer mugs were stacked high next to tapped kegs.

Siena had never been a huge drinker of beer at home. She and her mom were more sangria girls, but as she quickly looked around at the long tables nestled under the trees, she didn't see the diners drinking anything but beer. She'd have to give it a try.

"When in *Das Biergärten,* drink *Das Bier.*" Siena grinned, proud of the fact that she'd actually spoken three correct words in German. At least she had some of the vocab down.

They each took a half liter of Löwenbräu and made their way to a table underneath the shade of the chestnut trees. Every table around them was filled with people laughing and chatting. This was obviously where locals and tourists alike came to relax and enjoy themselves. Siena took a bite of her bratwurst and closed her eyes. The sausage, kraut, and potatoes were delicious together.

"Mmm," she mumbled, taking another bite, "this is the greatest combo. I can't believe I've gone my whole life without eating this stuff. My mom would never cook this at home."

"My mom cooks nothing but this type of stuff," Meg said as she dug into her own dish. "That's what happens when you have four teenage brothers. They're like locusts—they eat everything in their path!" She smiled at Siena's already half-empty plate. "You're a meat-and-potatoes girl, too."

"Must be the German in me," Siena said.

"You're German?" Meg asked.

"Half. My dad was."

"And he never cooked this for you?" Meg said.

Siena smiled, but she suddenly felt the bubble of

excitement she'd felt since she landed here deflate a little. "He died when I was a baby," she said.

"Oh, Siena," Meg said. "I'm sorry."

"That's rough," Chen said. "My dad's a total control freak, but I still like having the guy around."

"No worries," Siena said. "Hey, I'm probably way healthier for never having eaten bratwurst before, right?" She tried a casual laugh, but she still felt just the tiniest bit awkward. It was true, her mom never had been much into teaching her about her German heritage. But it had never really mattered much. Now she was learning about this whole other world that had belonged to her dad's family, so different from her world back home. What if she didn't fit in here at all?

"What's in this sausage, anyway?" Chen said, holding it up for inspection. "This is probably some sort of mystery meat. Have you ever seen sausage being made?"

"I have!" Meg piped up. "They take the intestines of the pigs first, you know, after the slaughter, and then—"

Siena gave Meg a gentle kick under the table.

"Don't think," Siena told Chen. "Just eat." She glanced at Meg's plate and saw a strange-looking piece of meat in the center. "Now *that* looks like mystery meat. What is it?"

"Schweinshaxn," Meg said.

"Oh, schweinshaxn! Of course! Why didn't I recognize it?" Siena said jokingly. "In English, please?"

"Pork knuckle," Meg said. "It's actually pretty tasty. I've had it before at home. There are a lot of Germans in Texas, believe it or not. Want to try?"

Siena grimaced, but then she remembered the bizarre foods her dad had tried that had made it into the Carpe Diem Hall of Fame. If he could do it, so could she. "Just a tiny bite," she said to Meg.

To her surprise, it wasn't all that bad—crispy on the outside with a juicy center and smoky flavor. Not great, but not totally gag-worthy, either.

"Your turn," she said to Chen.

"No way," Chen said. "I'll leave the experimental eating to you two."

"It's kind of cool that there's all these trees in the middle of the square like this," Siena said, looking around. "I always wondered why they were called beer gardens, and now I get it."

"They're chestnuts," Chen said, "planted to shade the cellars that the brewers kept their barrels in years ago."

Siena gaped at her. "How do you know all this?"

"Chen read her entire Munich guidebook cover to cover...twice," Meg said.

Siena just shook her head in awe.

"I have to take a break from bio every once in a while." Chen shrugged.

"Hey, if you've got the gift, put it to good use. And now we won't have to pay for a guided tour." She took a swig from her beer mug, waiting for the tartness to make her cringe. But the beer actually tasted great between bites of sausage and potatoes—the flavors all blending. It was like the world's most perfect comfort food, or Germany's anyway. Siena raised her mug to her new friends.

"Here's to an amazing semester in München," she said, clinking her mug to theirs.

"And to *Biergärtens*," Chen said.

"And to breaking rules," Meg said, giggling and giving Siena a nudge.

Siena smiled. A day and a half ago, she'd left the only home she'd ever known. But as she laughed and talked in the shady grove of chestnut trees, she thought maybe she could find a second one here.

Chapter Three

The next morning, Siena woke up to a knocking on her door.

"I'm up, Mom!" she yelled, wishing for the umpteenth time that Sweet Sara's didn't open so early on weekends. "You better have a cappuccino for me, and don't even think for a second I'm wearing the hairnet today!" She tumbled out of bed in the dark and opened the door to find Stefan standing there, wearing a huge grin and stifling laughter.

"Sorry," she said with a giggle. "I thought I was back in California for a second."

"In California, you don't have a roommate trying to sleep," a groggy Meg murmured from her bed.

After coming back to the dorm last night, she and Meg had stayed up until the wee hours talking. She'd tried to convince Chen to join in, but Chen said she had one thing on her mind—biology. She'd disappeared into her room, but not before promising she'd catch up with them sometime today.

Siena glanced at her travel alarm: 9:00 A.M. Ugh. No wonder her eyelids were still half-shut.

"Sorry, Meg. Go back to sleep," Siena whispered, and tiptoed into the hallway with Stefan, shutting the door behind her. Only then did she look down to discover she was still wearing the floor-length flowered flannel night-gown Meg had loaned her last night. Great. There was nothing about this situation that was at all flattering. Meanwhile, Stefan looked wide-awake and disarmingly gorgeous, those baby blues crystal clear and twinkling.

"I've never been called Mom before. A little frightening, actually. Maybe it's time for me to find a new job." He laughed. "And I don't have any cappuccino, but I do have something else to make up for that." He pointed down at her long-lost luggage.

"My stuff!" Siena cried.

"The airline dropped it off earlier this morning," Stefan said, handing it over.

"Earlier than nine A.M.? That's brutal," she said, stifling

a yawn. "Then I owe you double thanks. Thanks for my bag and thanks for not waking me up any earlier to give it to me."

"You're welcome on both accounts," Stefan said. "And now I'll let you get back to sleep." He started down the hallway, but then stopped and turned back to her. "One question for you. What is this hairnet? It sounds very interesting."

"I'll never tell," Siena said. The granny pj's she had on were bad enough. There was no way she was going to paint an even more disturbing picture of herself by explaining the horror that was a hairnet.

"I'll just look it up, then," Stefan said as he walked away grinning. "I have a feeling it's something I'd enjoy seeing."

"Not in this lifetime!" Siena called back with a laugh.

She hugged her bag happily. She was dying to open it up and dive into her own beloved clothes, but then thought she'd better wait until Meg was awake. She quietly let herself into her room, but just as soon as the door was safely shut, Meg threw back her covers and sat up, beaming widely.

"He so has a thing for you," she said giddily.

"Morning to you, too, Miss Sunshine." Siena smiled. "You sure are energetic for someone who was supposedly sleeping two minutes ago."

Meg blushed. "Okay, okay, so I wasn't sleeping...technically. I was just trying to get you out of the room so y'all could talk alone. There was definitely chemistry happening."

"He was just being nice. Or he was fantasizing about me in my to-die-for hairnet." She laughed. "I'm going with option number one."

Siena dumped her bag on her bed and flopped down next to it. Who was she kidding? She might be able to fool Meg for a little while, but the fact of the matter was that she was starting to crush on a lost cause. But when had her timing been right when it came to romance? Not when Brent Johnson moved in for a kiss and she turned her head at the last minute (the bruise on his forehead took weeks to go away), and certainly not when Toby Smith, the hottest guy at Ocean Vista High, had caught a glimpse of her at work in her full baking getup, hairnet and all. How was this time any different?

"He's sweet on you, Siena," Meg insisted enthusiastically. "He wouldn't joke like that with you unless he was. I can tell. Cody was like that when I first met him, too." She sighed happily. "Maybe you two will start dating in secret. That would be so romantic!"

"I could go for that," Siena said. "But who knows what'll happen? Even if he is flirting a little, and I'm not saying he is, he probably won't do anything about it. But if he does, I'll be more than happy to play along." She grinned and patted her bag. "In the meantime, at least I don't have to worry about blowing the rest of my budget on clothes, right?"

"I still can't believe you let your friend pack for you,"

Meg said. "How did you know she wouldn't pack all the wrong stuff?"

"I didn't." She laughed at Meg's horrified face. "But sometimes the best combos come from blending tastes." She unzipped her bag and was thrilled to see that Lizzie had packed some of her favorite outfits, although she couldn't help smiling at a couple of tiny tops Lizzie snuck in there with a note that read *Boy Magnets.*

Siena happily dressed in her own clothes and went downstairs to the computer lounge to write Lizzie a thank-you, leaving Meg completely absorbed in her laptop. There was already an e-mail from Lizzie waiting for her.

To: sagittarigurl@email.com

From: glamrific@email.com

Subject: Sulky in S.B.

Hey Senni,

You've been gone about two hours, and I'm writing from Sweet Sara's, where Foss and I are wallowing in self-pity over cups of decaf mocha. Your mom even refused to make us half-cafs. She said caffeine would only make our moods worse, and she doesn't want two morose teens on her hands. The prospect of going to school on Monday without you is a double-downer. Woe is us. If you'd like to

save us from diving off the pier, you know what to do. Dish!
We need details!

Miserably yours,

L

P.S. Moe the Knight is dressed in all black to mourn your
absence.

Siena replied, making sure to fill Lizzie and Foster in on
Stefan. *P.S.*, she added in her e-mail to Lizzie, *My new
friend Chen might be even more obsessed with shoes than
you are, if that's possible.* There. If news of Stefan didn't
cheer Lizzie up, info on a fellow fashionista would surely
do the trick.

While she was at the computer she figured this was a
great chance to concentrate on her plan to find Peter
Schwalm, too. She'd see if she could find a phone number
or address online for him.

The search engine popped up on the screen, and in just
a few minutes she had pulled up several German people-
finding sites. She typed in Peter Schwalm's name and
waited. No addresses found. But when she tried phone
numbers...she found him, all right—three hundred hims.
She scrolled through the list with a mixture of hopefulness
and exasperation. Her odds had just improved, but her
time line had been shot to Hades. Who knew Schwalm was

such a common name? She printed the list, then flipped through all sixteen pages of it. How long would it take her to call each number? And how many minutes would it use up on the international calling card she'd bought for her trip? She'd dumped a hefty sum from her meager budget into the card, and she needed to save most of it for calls home.

She didn't have time to try any numbers now, though, since last night she'd promised to give Meg an intro-to-yoga lesson before they left for the organized visit to the Residenz. Once Meg got a taste of it, Siena was convinced she'd be a yoga addict all the way. Back upstairs, she found Meg glued to her laptop (still!), an ear-to-ear grin plastered on her face.

"I'm almost ready for yoga!" Meg said to her, then she giggled as a message blipped onto her computer screen. "I just want to finish IM-ing Cody."

"Isn't it like four in the morning in Texas?" Siena asked, slipping her list of numbers in with the Carpe Diem List in her backpack.

"Yup." Meg giggled again. "He hasn't gone to bed yet. He was out last night with his friends."

"A partier, huh?" Siena teased. "How long have you been dating?"

"Hang on a sec." Meg typed one more sentence on her keyboard, smiled dreamily at the screen, then shut off her laptop. "Two and a half years," she said proudly.

"That's forever," Siena said. "It must be pretty serious."

"It is. I think, I mean, I hope it is." Meg blushed. "That's why I decided to make this trip. You know, while I still can."

"While you still *can*?" Siena asked, stretching out on the floor and starting her meditative breathing.

"Well, Cody's not big on leaving Texas and all, so I probably won't get to Europe much after high school, especially if we end up going to the same college." Meg sat down on the floor facing Siena. "And that's the plan."

"So you travel after college. Hey, you could do the whole backpacking thing. That'd be cool."

Meg nibbled on a nail and smiled shyly. "But if we stay together through college, well then, it could lead to..." Her whole face was turning strawberry now. "The M-word," she finished.

Siena's jaw dropped in disbelief. Meg's whole life was ahead of her, and she was already thinking about marriage? Siena could almost hear her mom now, rambling on about 1950s paternalistic brainwashing at work.

"Wow. I don't even have a *college* plan yet," Siena said. "I mean, college is a definite, but I have no idea *which* college. And the big M is an even bigger unknown."

"I don't think I have any unknowns in my life," Meg said worriedly.

"Well, you know what Bob Dylan said. A person is a success if she gets up in the morning and goes to bed at night, and in between does what she wants to do." Siena

tucked her hair behind her ears. "Stick with that, and you're good to go."

She folded her legs up close to her body and motioned Meg to do the same. "This is the primary Pawanmuktasana position in yoga." She placed her hands palms up on the floor. "Now," she said, "merge your spirit with the cosmic space." She closed her eyes and breathed in and out deeply, until she heard a half snort, half giggle from Meg. She cracked one eyelid to see Meg biting her lip, struggling not to laugh.

Meg smiled guiltily. "Sorry...I just have a hard time sitting still like this."

"Let's try a different asana," Siena said. "This is the Purna Titali—the full butterfly pose." She bent into place, then glanced over at Meg. Now she was the one who couldn't stop laughing. Meg looked more like a demented frog than a butterfly.

"What?" Meg said, sincerely this time. That made Siena laugh even harder, and then Meg cracked up, too.

"Maybe we should take a break," Siena said. "Why don't we finish decorating the room instead?"

Meg sighed with relief. "Sounds good to me. We have a couple hours before we're supposed to meet Dr. Goldstein for the tour anyway."

Pulling out their Friday shopping booty, they set to work. Siena draped a couple of ocean blue scarves she'd bought over the nightstands and hung her wind chime from the ceiling. Meg's Tibetan throw pillows added some exotic flair, and her vintage posters were the perfect accents.

"Voilà," Siena said as she hung the last strand of aqua beads across the window. The eclectic room was full of warmth and flavor now.

"It looks amazing," Meg said. "I love it!"

"What did I tell you?" Siena said. "When in doubt— blend. It changes everything." She smiled at Meg, glad that she'd gotten her for a roomie. And if this was Meg's one-and-only shot at Europe, Siena was going to make sure it was the trip of a lifetime.

That afternoon, still beaming from the makeover they'd given their room, the girls took a tour of the Residenz with the other program students. The huge royal palace had been home to the most important Bavarian rulers from the fourteenth century until World War I, and it was only a few minutes' walk from the Lebenhaus. With its sand-colored exterior and long, rectangular shape, the Residenz didn't strike Siena as particularly grandiose until they stepped inside. The gilded ceilings and elaborate wall-to-wall paintings and furniture all glittered richly.

"Not too shabby," Chen whispered as they wandered through the rooms. "I could live like this."

"You've got the shoes for it," Siena said, admiring the new Prada flats Chen was wearing with her jeans.

"And for half the price." Chen smiled.

· "I'd miss the big open Texas sky if I lived in a palace with gold ceilings," Meg said.

"This place isn't for me, either," Siena said. "I'd trip over one of those million-dollar Oriental rugs and smash into the nearest porcelain cabinet. Sadly, even yoga hasn't helped my coordination much."

"This palace was home to a number of the Wittelsbach royal family for close to five hundred years," Dr. Goldstein explained as she led the group through the Ancestral Gallery. "You'll see that some of these family portraits have tears in the canvas that have been repaired. During World War Two, the Nazis, in haste, cut the paintings out of the frames to hide them. They were all returned after the war ended."

Siena wandered around the room and then into the Antiquarium, a huge, long hallway lined with frescoes and busts of Greek and Roman heroes. She caught sight of Stefan just inside the entrance, studying the frescoes along the ceiling. Her heart started pounding at the sight of him. Even his Adam's apple looked cute from this angle. She started to wave to him, but then she saw that on his other side was Briana, practically leaning her head against his shoulder as she looked up at the paintings high above.

"Sometimes they hold banquets and concerts in this hall," Stefan was saying to Briana.

"I've heard they're incredible," Briana said. "My father's been to a few when he's traveled here on business." She gave her hair a glamgirl toss. "Tell me more about this painting?" she singsonged, leaning in closer.

Stefan smiled and began to enthusiastically explain the history behind the frescoes. He seemed to be enjoying his role as mentor, and Siena wasn't entirely convinced his animated face and quick smile stemmed from a love of art. Briana was determined, that much was for sure. Siena guessed that she was also used to getting whatever she wanted, whenever she wanted it. On one hand, she could almost understand how Stefan might get sucked into Briana's doe-eyed routine, in spite of his job. On the other, he seemed way too grounded to fall for that. Didn't he? She couldn't figure it out, and trying was exhausting, so she turned away to track down Meg and Chen.

She caught up with them as they headed toward the Reliquary Room, next up on the tour. Briana sauntered up just then, too, stationing herself right next to Dr. Goldstein.

"Does anyone know what's housed in this next room?" Dr. Goldstein asked the group.

"Relics supposedly from the holy land," Briana said in about a nanosecond.

Siena had to laugh at Briana's persistence. The girl seemed to have only two MOs: kissing up to Dr. Goldstein and hitting on Stefan. And so far, she was succeeding in both.

"Thank you, Briana." Dr. Goldstein nodded approvingly. "You're absolutely right. Here, you can see the bones of

saints, and even two of the infants slaughtered when King Herod ordered the deaths of all firstborn sons in hopes of killing Jesus."

"Gruesome," Chen said. "This is the type of stuff Shakespeare would write about...death on display. Let's go check out poor Yorick."

"I don't know..." Meg said, peering uncertainly into the room. "I have a sensitive stomach."

"Spoken like a true pork-knuckle eater," Chen said. "You're coming." She locked elbows with Meg and playfully pulled her through the doorway.

Siena peeked around the door to see a tiny room full of ornate rings and jeweled relics, all displayed by being worn on skulls and various other bones. Meg and Chen were already staring, fascinated, into one of the cases where a skull lay covered with a velvet, jeweled cap. Siena planted herself firmly outside in the hallway.

"Don't you want to go in?" a voice said from behind her.

She turned to see Stefan, smiling at her. "No way," she whispered. "I know bad karma when I see it."

"It is morbid," Stefan acknowledged. "*Bitte*, please, let me take you somewhere a little more cheerful."

He led her outside to a quiet, enclosed courtyard he called the Grotto Court. She gasped when she saw that a whole wall of the courtyard was covered in tiny seashells. There was a shell mosaic of a mermaid, Medusa's head, and the god Mercury.

"Now this is way more my style." She smiled. "Mythology and Mother Nature in perfect harmony. I knew it was just a matter of time before I saw Germany's pagan side."

"When it was first built in the fifteen-hundreds, red wine poured out of the wall and into the fountains," Stefan said.

"There must have been some wild parties thrown here back then." She laughed.

"The entire grotto was destroyed in bombings during the war," Stefan said. "But the Nazis had taken photos of it. So when the war ended, even though Bavarians had no money, they wanted to rebuild the grotto. They collected all the shells that you see here by hand and gradually re-created the mosaic."

"This whole thing?" Siena cried. "That's amazing."

They were still staring at the beautiful handiwork when the rest of the group burst into the courtyard, talking and laughing. Briana and her clique, Stacy and Kim, made a beeline for Stefan and immediately started asking questions. When was the grotto built? What kind of shells were used? Who was that woman with the snake hair?

Stefan answered each one patiently as Siena got more and more irked. Logic told her that he was only doing his job, and that he'd just been answering her own questions minutes before. Still, her own interest had been genuine, and Briana's naïve Barbie routine was getting old. But what right did she have getting all worked up about Briana

anyway? It wasn't like she stood any better chance with Stefan, did she?

As Dr. Goldstein rounded up everyone to head back to the dorm, Briana and company followed Stefan out into the Residenzstrasse. Siena told herself to stop all this pointless obsessing about Stefan. But it was a lot easier for her head to tell that to her heart than for her heart to listen. Once class started on Monday, though, she thought she'd be so busy that she'd barely even see him. Or Briana (she hoped). Siena shrugged off her moodiness and caught up with Meg and Chen, who were in the middle of a debate over whether or not the finger bones they'd seen had really been those of John the Baptist.

"It's not scientifically possible," Chen said. "The bones would have disintegrated centuries ago."

"Maybe not...if they really *were* a saint's," Meg said. "They could have survived, you know, miraculously or something."

"Not possible," Chen said firmly. "Siena, tell her."

Siena thought about Stefan, and the slim chance, if any, she had of dating him. She thought about Peter Schwalm, and the even slimmer chance she had of finding him. Then she smiled at her friends. "I am a firm believer in infinite possibilities. Especially this semester."

Chapter Four

To: glamrific@email.com
From: sagittarigurl@email.com
Subject: Mystery Man of Munich

Lizzie,

Thanks for the e-mails. Nope, no new developments on the Stefan front. Give a girl more than twenty-four hours to work her magic, will ya? ☺ Of course breaking the rule to date him is no big deal to me. If he were giving me the greenlight, I'd go for it. (You know I would.) But until I get

a sign from him, we're in limboland. I'll keep you posted.

Senni

A bitter wind blew across the front lawn of the Universität München on Monday morning, and Siena tucked her hands even deeper into her coat pockets.

"This is even colder than Boston," Chen hissed through chattering teeth. "I can't believe Meg gets to sleep an extra hour before her first class while we freeze. Am I wrong, or did they tell us this was *spring* semester?"

Siena blew a puff of air out of her mouth and smiled up at the crisp clear sky. "I love it! We never have weather like this in Santa Barbara. My cold-weather self embraces it."

"My cold-weather self wants a portable heater," Chen grumbled. "Let's pick up the pace. I want to get to my first class before hypothermia sets in. Which building are you in for European history?"

Siena reached into her bag for her class schedule. Her hand fumbled around inside—there was her notebook, her Post-its, the daily horoscope she'd printed out from the net, her purple glitter gel pen, a clump of old receipts (as in *last year* old), and scribbled reminder notes, but no schedule. "I'm positive I put it in here this morning…." she mumbled. Well, she was pretty sure she had, at least.

"How would you find it in all that even if you did?" Chen teased. "Don't tell me you forgot it."

"*Forgot* is a strong word." Siena giggled. "Temporarily misplaced is more like it."

"Well," Chen said, stopping in front of a small brick building, "This is me. Dr. Goldstein teaches my first class, you know. Maybe she has a copy of the schedules."

Sure enough, when Siena followed Chen inside and asked, Dr. Goldstein told her that she had copies of everyone's schedule. "Don't worry," she said kindly. "It happens all the time on the first day of classes."

Siena thanked her, smiled at Chen, and then sprinted to her history class, throwing herself into a seat in the back just as the campus bell tower finished tolling eight o'clock. She grabbed her horoscope from her bag and quickly scanned through it—there was no way she could wrap her head around the history of the world until she tapped into her astrological touchstone. She was happy to see that *even though there may be a few bumps in the road to start,* her *moon sign would ensure good fortune later in the week.* So forgetting her schedule was just a minor bump.

"Excuse me," a girl's voice said next to her. "Are you Siena?"

Siena looked over to see two familiar-looking girls sitting next to her.

"That's me," Siena said. "You're in the Intercultural Program, too, right? I saw you guys at the Residenz on Saturday."

The redheaded girl nodded, smiling. "I'm Mia, and this is Chrissy." She pointed to a girl with cropped chestnut hair. "We met Meg yesterday in the caf, and she mentioned you were her roommate. We're here through the S.A.S.S. program, too."

"Cool!" Siena nodded, then noticed Mia peering over her shoulder at the horoscope on her desk. "Hey," Siena said. "I'm just reading my horoscope. Do you want to hear yours?"

Mia grinned as Chrissy said, "Sure."

"Great," she said, thrilled to be sharing news from the astral plane. "So, what're your signs?"

Siena was just starting a rundown of their zodiac personality traits when Dr. Schultz walked in to begin class. His full white beard and crinkled-up eyes would have made him a dead ringer for Santa Claus, except for the fact that he seemed incapable of smiling. Instead, he offered up a somber frown as a hello. Siena was nearly nodding off during his welcome address when she shifted her eyes from the podium and caught sight of Briana and Stacy. They were sitting front and center in the first row, overeagerly listening to Dr. Schultz. So much for her theory that she wouldn't be seeing much of Briana in class. Well, at least she'd picked a seat in the back.

As she struggled with Dr. Schultz's in-depth introduction to the class syllabus, she scribbled haphazard notes on Post-its. An essay due every other week...check. A midterm research paper making up 30 percent of her grade...check. A final research paper making up another 40...crap.

Okay, so she wouldn't be taking one of her occasional ditch days in European history, that was for sure. She had perfected the art of the ditch to the beach back home with Lizzie and their friends, and she'd hoped to get a Euroditch or two in here. But this was only one class. She could surely fit in a little midday hiatus from her German class, or maybe even math, especially when the weather turned warmer (if it ever did).

As class wrapped up, she leaned over to Chrissy and Mia. "Tomorrow I'll show you how to interpret your sun signs," she told them.

"Cool," Mia said. "I always wanted to know more about astrology. If all of Dr. Schultz's lectures are as boring as the one today, we'll definitely need the distraction."

Siena grabbed her bag and headed for the door. The room was quickly clearing out, but Briana and Stacy were still standing near the doorway, chatting away.

"I know he's not available...technically," Siena overheard Briana saying as she walked by. "But a few minutes with him to myself, and we'll see about that."

Stacy gave a high-pitched giggle. "I can't wait to hear the details."

Siena stifled a laugh as she breezed past them. What did Briana think this was, a reality-TV show? There was no way Stefan would fall that easily... she hoped.

She stepped outside, pulled out the map of campus, and checked her surroundings. There were a number of stately, red-roofed academic buildings surrounding her, and she had no idea which one her German-language class was in. She randomly picked a direction and headed across a wide cobblestone square. It was sheer luck that, five minutes later, she stumbled onto a grand building with huge white columns and the word LINGUISTIK carved into its facade.

With great relief, she found her classroom and sat down, only to be presented with a first-day pop quiz, or *unangekuendigter test,* as her prof, Dr. Steinberg, called it. The test was supposedly to "assess skills," which she quickly discovered she didn't have...at all. The other kids in her class, a mix of local Gymnasium students and kids from her program, seemed to be blowing right through the quiz. A few even turned it in with fifteen minutes to spare. She, on the other hand, didn't have a clue how to string together more than two sentences in German, let alone whole paragraphs.

After reluctantly turning in her quiz, she checked the time on the clock tower looming over the campus. It was already after 1:00 P.M., and she was starving. At the edge of a wide lawn near the clock tower, she stumbled upon a little campus café. Luckily, she grabbed one of the few remaining seats inside, away from the cold. She ordered a bierwurst sandwich (more sausage!) and something called kartoffelsalat, which she discovered was a delicious form of potato salad. As she ate, she pasted even more Post-its into her notebook for more German test dates. This was getting the teeniest bit complicated. Her notebook was practically drowning in Post-its.

By the time she collapsed into a chair in her last class of the day, film, she was out of breath and nearly out of enthusiasm. She'd had to run to this class after leaving her schedule in the girls' bathroom and racing back to get it. Her organizational skills had always been pretty sketchy, she was the first to admit, but come on. To forget her schedule twice in one day was ridiculous—even for her. She did perk up a little bit when Dr. Nielson walked into the room. His glasses had electric blue frames, and together with his mustache and beret, they made him look artistic and a touch eccentric. Siena liked him already.

After giving the class a passionate fifteen-minute introduction into the art of film, he started a DVD demonstration of their semester project. The project was to create an experimental film on the "German experience." Siena wasn't entirely sure what the German experience was yet, but she had the whole semester to figure that out. At least that was a good thing.

"Seventy-five percent of your grade will be based on

this final project," he explained as images flashed across the screen. "I don't seek convention. I seek eccentricity, singularity. I seek you…each of you, in your final piece on Germany." Dr. Nielson froze the screen on a black-and-white image of a cooper dancing with a skeletal figure beneath a strobe light. "This was shot at Oktoberfest and then later manipulated with Claymation. Not an unusual setting, but an extraordinary interpretation of the mundane."

For the next half hour, Siena stared at the film clips and felt her heart pick up the pace. This was all fascinating, but for it to count toward 75 percent of her grade was huge. What was it with these classes and their supersized projects, papers, and exams?

"Good luck on your journey of self-exploration," Dr. Nielson said. "You'll each have a digital camcorder at your disposal for the duration of the semester. This is the tool of your craft. You may pick it up on your way out." He flipped on the overhead lights and students bustled toward the door, each taking a camcorder from a table at the front of the room as they went.

Siena breathed a sigh of relief. She'd survived day one. As she stood to go, she noticed a black-garbed, goateed guy stooped over a camcorder at his desk. He was staring at the camcorder screen with an intense look that practically screamed "tortured artist." He reminded Siena of a few of her more deep-thinking, Shakespearean-tragedy-type friends from back home.

"Working already?" she asked, pausing next to his desk.

He looked up from his camcorder somberly.

"I have my own camera," he said with a German accent. "My third eye." He tapped his forehead with utter seriousness. "I've been working on this piece for a while."

"Can I take a look?" she asked.

He hesitated for just a second, then handed the camera over to her. A demonic-looking dancing puppet split into a kaleidoscope of shards on the camcorder screen. Words floated across the screen, superimposed on the images. "I shot it at the Munich City Museum in the puppetry exhibit," he said. "I'm from here, so I can spend a lot of time at the museums."

"What are the words on the screen?" Siena asked.

"Heinrich Heine's poetry," he said. "It represents the split that oppression causes in identity."

"Wow," Siena said. "That's definitely a singular form of cinema."

"It's not cinema," he said defensively. "It's cinemart."

"Cinemart," she corrected with a smile. "That suits it much better. I'm Siena."

"Ansel." He nodded, grabbing his bag and heading for the door.

She walked out into the hall with him, picking up her

assigned camcorder on the way. She was swinging it by its strap when Ansel lunged for it.

"Don't strangle it," he said. "Cradle it." He held it up for her, pointing to tiny buttons. "This is record, rewind, pause, play."

"Got it," she said, ever so gently settling the camcorder into her bag. "Well, Ansel, I'll catch you later. I'd love to see more of the Marionette's Midlife Crisis next class."

"Hey," he said thoughtfully as he walked away. "That's not a bad title."

Siena left the building with a new sense of purpose. All right, this was more her cup of tea. She knew she could do experimental film. Maybe not quite so warped as a psycho-puppetry show, but a little color, a little spice, and she'd have something cheerier that just might work.

A few hours of failed color and spice later, and Siena was logging onto the net back at Lebenhaus. So much for her self-proclaimed skills as a film producer. She'd made her first attempt at filming right after class when she met up with Meg and Chen in the Englischer Garten, a huge park full of lawns, trees, and wooded paths. The chilly morning had turned into a slightly less chilly day, and the sun was shining. Siena wanted to give her camcorder a try, so she'd filmed Meg and Chen walking and talking and laughing in the park.

Now, back at the dorm, she'd run the DVD in the computer lab to discover she hadn't caught anything on film but blackness. The reason for that was as much a mystery to her as the German-verb-conjugation homework she had pushed off to the side in favor of checking her e-mail.

To: sagittarigurl@email.com
From: yogamama@email.com
Subject: My little jetsetter

Hi sweetie,

Thanks for the message last night. I already miss my yoga partner! I realized I forgot to give you this phone number (attached) before you left. A few gray hairs and I can't remember anything! The number is for your dad's cousin. She lives just outside of Munich. I only met her once at our wedding years ago. I don't think she speaks English well, but I thought you might want to have her phone number, just in case. This way, you know there's family close by. Okay, enough maternal mush. I'm off to Tae Bo.

Love,

Mom

She printed out the address for her dad's cousin Anna Schlegel before she logged off. She'd have to try giving her a call while she was here, but not until she got a firmer grasp of the German language. It could be the first step toward getting to know her dad's side of the family. Anna

might even know something about what had happened to Peter. She really needed to start working on her phone list of Peter Schwalms soon, too. First things first, though; she had those German conjugations and a camcorder to wrestle with. After that, a few phone calls would be a *Stück* of cake. Or was it a *Stücken*?

By the time her first tutoring session with Chen rolled around midweek, Siena had given up hope of any potential ditch days this semester. With this regimen, she'd be lucky to keep her scholarship even with perfect class attendance. She hadn't even had time to make one single phone call on her Peter Schwalm list, since most of her waking moments were spent trying to get a handle on her new workload.

"Dr. Goldstein wasn't kidding when she said the Gymnasium was going to be challenging," she told Chen as she opened her German textbook. "A torture chamber is more like it."

Chen rolled her eyes over the top of her own German book, where she was scribbling away on another sheet of paper, probably taking meticulous notes. "No moaning allowed. We have work to do."

Siena threw in one exaggerated groan for good measure, then pulled out her notebook. They'd decided to hold the tutoring session in Chen's room, since Meg had been totally absorbed in a whispery phone conversation with

Cody in Siena's room, and Siena wanted to give them some privacy. After seeing Chen's room, she had to admit she'd had the girl pegged all wrong. Chen was a neat freak, just like Siena had guessed, but she was also neat chic. Her closet was color-coordinated, with hangers each one inch apart, but her clothes were straight out of *Vogue*.

"Shopaholics Anonymous," Chen said when she'd noticed Siena's bulging eyes.

Siena found herself wishing she could convince Chen to put on a fashion show for her instead of tutoring. Anything would be better than embarking on an hour of math and German. But Chen looked determined, and Siena was all out of angst ammo and excuses.

"Come on," Chen said, leaving her book on the bed and sitting down on the floor next to Siena. "Let's get started."

"Don't you need your book, too?" Siena asked. "To write down your conjugations?"

"I already did them, so we can share your book."

Siena stared at her. "But you just got the assignment this afternoon. When did you have time?"

Chen blushed ever so slightly. "Last week."

"What?" Siena cried. "How? Spill it."

Chen shrugged, looking a little uncomfortable. "All right!" She threw up her hands. "I have a photographic memory, okay? I read through the textbooks before the semester started so I wouldn't have to study as much."

Siena grinned. "I cannot believe I have a genius at my

disposal! I knew my good fortune would kick in late this week!"

"Huh?"

"Horoscope. Never mind," Siena said. "But why carry around all those books if you've got a blueprint of that stuff in your head already?" She pulled Chen's German book off the bed, and a piece of paper fluttered out onto the ground. "You don't even need to take all these notes."

She glanced down at the paper on the floor, guessing it was probably the secret to time travel or the cure for cancer or something. But instead, she saw what looked like lines of verse.

"Okay," Chen said. "You've outed me. It's poetry."

"Oops," Siena said. "I'm sorry. I didn't mean to pry."

Chen shrugged. "Well, now you know my secret passion. This…and shoes."

"I knew that one already." Siena smiled.

"One of the reasons I wanted to study abroad here was because of Heinrich Heine, my favorite poet."

"That's the second time I've heard that name this week," Siena said.

"Not surprising. He's a pretty famous German," Chen said.

"But what's with hiding the poetry in your textbooks?"

"A habit I learned in Boston," Chen admitted. "My parents aren't very open-minded about me being a doctor *and* a poet, so I got used to hiding the poems. Now I can't get inspired to write in anything else. Call it poet's block. How's that for irony?"

"Hey." Siena smiled. "I'm just glad you're in touch with your inner muse."

"I like to keep a low profile, so don't let it get around," Chen said with a grin. "I own stilettos and I'm not afraid to use them." She slipped her poetry back into her book. "Now let's deal with this." She picked up Siena's notebook, and a mass of Post-its spilled out of it.

"They're for my essay and exam dates," Siena explained when faced with Chen's skeptical glance. "It worked fine for me back home, but here...well, there's too many tests and papers to keep track of." She shrugged. "I guess I'm every anal-retentive person's nightmare, huh?"

"You won't be by the time I'm through with you," Chen said, handing Siena a small black binder. "Your very own calendar. A gift to welcome you to my world. It's time to let the Post-its go."

"Do you always keep spare calendars handy?" Siena teased.

"I'm *always* prepared." Chen smiled.

"Thanks." Siena flipped through the calendar, staring at the structured tabs and hour-by-hour lines for scheduling. She wasn't a by-the-book kind of girl, but that seemed to be the only way to do things here. Still, she couldn't help feeling that a timetabled life would be much easier said than done.

Chapter Five

To: sagittarigurl@email.com
From: fossybear@email.com
Subject: Lizzie the Psycho Cupid

Sweet Senni,

Happy Valentine's Day! Lizzie decided to hold our annual Valentine's Schmalentine's beach party, even though it won't be the same without you. She's giving me a hard time about not having a date for the party, but I told her if she said one more word about it, she had to give my iPod back. It worked. She didn't mention it at all today, and I may never see my iPod again. Oh well. I knew when she said she wanted to "borrow" it, I was taking my chances.

Foster

P.S. Attached is a pic of Moe decked out for Valentine's Day. Behold, the world's only cross-dressing knight. (The boa and leather bra were Lizzie's idea.)

The following Monday, as soon as Dr. Schultz finished up his way long, way boring lecture in European history, Siena folded up the small zodiac chart she'd brought to share with Chrissy and Mia and slid it into her bag. Since they sat in the back of the room, it was easy to slip in a little harmless extracurricular activity while Dr. Schultz talked, but they only resorted to it during especially excruciating lessons.

"Sorry, guys," she whispered as they looked at her forlornly. "He's about to give our papers back."

She was really psyched to see the grade for her first history paper—a short essay on "something of historical significance to the modern German people." Her topic had been a stroke of genius from the celestial plane as far as she was concerned, and man, had she slaved away at writing it.

She twirled her bangles nervously, watching Dr. Schultz pull the stack of papers from his briefcase. This was a first

for her, feeling stressed about a class, of all things! It didn't help that Briana, sitting pretty with Stacy, had just gotten her paper back and was beaming.

Dr. Schultz put Siena's paper facedown on her desk. When she turned it over, she couldn't believe the big red *C* at the top.

Dr. Schultz had written a note: *Siena, while your discussion of the German maypole as a fertility symbol in ancient rites of spring was certainly intriguing, I hope your next essay reflects a more grounded understanding of this country's past.*

Siena took a few calming breaths. So much for points for originality.

"Not what you were hoping for?" Mia asked her.

Siena held up her grade for the girls to see. "Well, ladies," she said, shouldering her bag and raising her chin with new determination. "Never let it be said that the system conquered Siena Bernstein. As my mom always says, 'If the mountain won't come to Muhammad, Muhammad better have some kick-ass hiking boots handy.'"

"Who's Muhammad?" Mia asked, but Siena was already on her way out the door. She needed reinforcements, and she needed them now.

"You wrote about *what*?" her first reinforcement (a.k.a. Chen) said. Siena had just finished recounting the whole story to her and Meg over lunch in the cafeteria.

"I still don't understand the connection between maypoles and fertility," Meg said.

Chen leaned over and whispered in her ear, and suddenly Meg broke into fits of giggles. "Oh! Now I get it."

"I thought my idea was very creative." Siena sniffed.

"There's no doubt about that." Chen laughed.

"Don't worry, hon," Meg said, giving her shoulder a comfort pat. "You'll do better on the next one."

"Look," Chen said. "Expectations are high here. You're smart. Just give them what they want. Straightforward, to the point, and always avoid anything that would make a professor blush."

Siena sighed. "All right," she said. "I'll try. But boring isn't in my nature." Then she giggled. "I betcha Dr. Schultz never looks at the maypole in the Viktualienmarkt the same way again."

The next afternoon Siena discovered that, sadly, history wasn't the only thing she didn't get about this country. If there was ever a time when being fluent in German would have come in handy, this would be it. She hung up the pay phone in the student lounge and stared in frustration at the list of phone numbers for Peter Schwalm. She'd finally had time to make a few tentative phone calls from her list. The calls were not going well, to say the least.

The first three phone numbers she tried were disconnected. Two more phone numbers, and people answered

the phone, but none of them spoke any English at all, and Siena couldn't get past *Sprechen Sie Englisch?*

She tentatively lifted the receiver again, deciding to make one last call. She was relieved when a man's voice answered with "Hello" instead of *"Guten Tag."*

"Hello," she said. *"Sprechen Sie Englisch?"*

"Yes," he said.

"Oh, thank God!" Siena cried. "May I speak to Peter Schwalm?"

"You've got him," he said.

Clutching the receiver, Siena fumbled through her dad's story. After she was done, there was a long silence on the other end of the line. She held her breath and waited.

"I'm sorry," the man finally said. "I'd love to help you. But I'm not the guy you're looking for."

Of course he couldn't be, she immediately scolded herself for getting her hopes up. *Her* Peter Schwalm wouldn't use a word like *guy* or speak perfect English without an accent. This particular Peter Schwalm, she found out over the course of the phone call, was only nineteen and had just moved to Berlin *from* America. What were the chances! She thanked Peter for his time and hung up the phone.

She grabbed her list and stomped upstairs to her room. So far she was six for six in the failed calls category, and if she didn't improve her German soon, her odds wouldn't improve any, either. She threw open her door and slammed it behind her.

Startled, Meg looked up from her laptop. "What's wrong?"

"I can't do anything right this week!" Siena cried. "First, my history paper, and now..." Her voice trailed off as she sighed. "It's a long story."

Meg was immediately at her side. "Okay. We've got all night. Do you want to talk about it? Or maybe do some yoga? I'll give it another try."

Siena shook her head. "Thanks, but I am just way too off balance for that, with all this negative energy."

Meg grabbed her coat and purse, turned off her laptop without even so much as a final e-farewell to Cody, and headed for the door. "Get your coat. You are in desperate need of some strudel. I'll get Chen, and then we're out of here."

An hour later at Café-Konditorei Schneller, their recently discovered hangout for munchies between and after classes, Siena finished her last bite of piping-hot strudel, and with it, the whole story behind her dad and the Carpe Diem List and Peter Schwalm. Over a cup of steaming buttergrog, a German version of spiced apple cider, she'd managed to put a stop to her drama-queen episode.

The comforting buzz of quiet conversations, the easy

laughter popping up here and there—the whole laid-back atmosphere in the café reminded her of Sweet Sara's. Somehow, that made her words come easier. Before she started talking, she had guessed Meg and Chen would understand the need for her search for Peter. She was so glad she had been right. They understood everything.

"That is so amazing," Meg said after Siena finished her story. "Just think. If Peter had been caught helping your dad and grandparents escape, your dad would never have met your mom. You might never have been born at all!" She actually looked close to tears herself. "You have to find him."

"Definitely," Chen agreed, sipping her cider. "How many phone numbers did you say you have?"

"About three hundred," Siena said.

Chen groaned. "There has to be a better way."

"Do you know where your grandparents lived in Berlin?" Meg asked. "Some of their old neighbors might know something. Or how about addresses for old friends?"

Siena shook her head, sensing some of the relief she'd felt right after telling them start to fade away.

"Or coworkers?" Chen asked. "Where did your grandfather work?"

"I don't know!" Siena said. "Look, I barely know anything about my dad's family. The Carpe Diem List is just about all I know about *him*."

Maybe it hadn't been such a good idea to tell Meg and Chen about this after all. It wasn't that she didn't want their help, but who was she kidding? The truth was, her dad's life was almost a total mystery to her. Now her Carpe Diem List didn't seem like much at all.

"It's okay, Siena," Meg said quietly. "We'll figure it out."

"Yeah," Chen said. "Don't get your 'aura' all out of whack."

"Chen!" Siena said, brightening. "So you actually believe in auras now?"

"No way," Chen said. "I was just hoping it would distract you."

"You know, my mom did give me the phone number for my dad's cousin Anna Schlegel. She lives close to here and might be able to help." Siena paused, then figured she might as well just admit it. "I've kind of been avoiding calling her, though."

"Why? She's family!" Meg said. "Maybe she'd be able to tell you something else about your dad."

"She probably doesn't even know who I am. And she doesn't speak English," Siena said miserably. "Face it. My German sucks. Tonight's phone calls were proof of that."

"True," said Chen, "but I'm fixing that. We just need a little more time."

"Y'all can't wait around for Siena to get fluent. It'll take forever," Meg said.

"Thanks. No pressure or anything, Meg," Siena moaned.

"Sorry," Meg said. "But I bet Anna will be happy to hear from you. And this is way too important for you to wait."

Siena hated to admit it, but Meg had a point. The semester was already a few weeks old. She couldn't afford to waste any time.

"But how am I supposed to talk to her if I do call now?" she said.

They all went silent at that, and she dug into the second piece of strudel she'd ordered. There was nothing like two helpings of dessert to release negative energy.

"I'll help you," Chen said quietly, keeping her eyes on the table. "We'll make the calls together."

"Really?" Siena nearly choked midchew, but recovered in time to give Chen a big hug. "Thank you! Thank you! Thank you!"

Chen squirmed out from under Siena's hug and straightened her top. "Careful," she said with mock sternness. "This is a Chanel knockoff I'm especially proud of." But a smile broke across her face even as the words left her mouth.

Back at the Lebenhaus, Siena headed for the student lounge for the second time that night, this time with Chen and with a new sense of optimism. Using Siena's calling card, Chen dialed Anna Schlegel's number. Siena sat down on the edge of the couch, waiting anxiously for Chen to show some sign that the call had gone through.

"Is it ringing?" Siena whispered excitedly. "Can you hear anything?"

"I might be able to if you kept quiet," Chen said, rolling her eyes.

"Sorry."

Chen put her mouth over the receiver and whispered, "Her answering machine just came on." She left a message for Anna, giving her Siena's e-mail address and the main number for the Lebenhaus, and Siena even chimed in a hello.

"What if she doesn't call?" she asked after Chen hung up the phone. "What if she doesn't want to meet me?"

"For someone who puts so much faith in cosmic forces," Chen said, "you sure don't have a lot of faith in people at the moment." She smiled at Siena. "She'll call. And we'll find Peter Schwalm."

Siena nodded, grateful to Chen for being willing to help, and for keeping her a little more grounded.

"Now," Chen said. "I have some depressing poetry to compose in my room. I'll see you later." She turned to leave.

"Chen, wait!" Siena called out. "Thanks," she said to her. And she meant it with all her heart.

Siena didn't feel tired at all yet, even though it was getting late, so she logged on in the computer lounge to kill

some time. There was an e-mail from Lizzie, and Siena smiled as she read, *How's the search for Peter going? How's Stefan the Great? If this guy really looks like Heath Ledger, I'm on the next plane to Germany.* But even after she poured her heart out to Lizzie in a long e-mail, sleep wouldn't come easily for her.

Too many thoughts raced through her head—about her father, Peter, the tough time she seemed to be having finding her place in this country. She lay in bed reading through the Carpe Diem List until she started nodding off. Then she tacked it up onto her headboard and closed her eyes, hoping that if Anna did get in touch with her, maybe she'd have some of the answers that she was looking for.

Chapter Six

Siena grabbed another film container from the cart next to her scanner and popped it open, wondering just how long she'd been down here in the dank, musty bowels of the university library. She didn't have a watch on, not that she ever wore one anyway, but she guessed she'd been searching through the periodical archives for a couple hours already. After her Friday classes ended, she'd grabbed a cup of Kaffee from the campus café and made her way to the ivy-covered research library, with its grand, three-story brick facade. Tomorrow morning she was leaving for a two-day program bus tour of the Romantic Road,

an ancient trade route that had now become one of Germany's most traveled scenic roads. So she wanted to use her few hours of free time this afternoon to try another search tactic for finding Peter Schwalm. If Peter had been arrested after he helped her dad and grandparents get out of Berlin, there might be some newspaper articles giving information about him. She might even be able to look into prison records, if she had to.

The archives librarian had been nice enough to show her how to use microfiche, rolls of miniature film that could be projected into a readable size using these clunky machines with huge screens. She'd explained that all the newspapers had been stored on microfiche because the hard copies were too fragile to touch.

Siena scanned through another old newspaper from West Germany. She'd given East German papers a try, too, but they had been censored, so their pages held more Communist propaganda than accurate information. This particular paper was full of accounts of arrests and shootings at the Wall. It was all so disheartening. And it took forever to get through each paper because she had such a hard time reading in German. If she didn't see sunlight soon, she was in serious danger of shriveling up under mounds of dust-covered film canisters, never to be seen or heard from again.

It had been two weeks since she'd left the message on Anna's machine, and she hadn't heard from her yet. She and Chen had been diligently going through the list of phone numbers every night. So far, after hours on the phone, they had knocked out about fifty numbers, without any luck. Some of the people they'd spoken to were very kind, showing a genuine interest in Siena's story, but none of them were able to give any information on the man she was looking for.

"This isn't as simple as I'd thought it would be," she had told Chen the other night, after yet another failed phone session.

"Well, you're looking for a guy your family lost track of almost half a century ago," Chen said. "Considering what we have to work with, I think we're making progress."

"I didn't expect it to take so much time," Siena said. "Don't feel like you have to keep helping me."

"Hey," Chen said, "I never do anything I don't feel like doing."

"But that's what I don't get," Siena said. "Why do you even want to help me with this? You could be spending this time writing or doing so many other things."

"And miss out on all this quality bonding time with you? Never!" Chen smiled, then suddenly got serious. "Look. My parents immigrated to America from China. It took them years to be able to leave the country. My dad came to America first, and then sent for my mom five years later."

"I can't imagine what that must have been like," Siena had whispered.

"From what they've told me, it was no joyride," Chen said. "But the point is ... they could have used a friend like Peter, you know?"

Siena nodded.

"All right," Chen finally said. "No more digging around in my past. We have some serious calling-card mileage to make tonight."

That had been several days ago, and still no luck. Siena skimmed one final paper until her eyes blurred. Not one mention of Peter Schwalm anywhere. The more she read, the more she wondered ... not just about her dad's childhood, but about her grandparents' lives. Theirs was so different from her carefree life at home. It sure put her struggles with classes and guys in perspective.

She carefully returned all of the microfiche containers to their drawers, packed up, and headed back to the dorm. So the library hadn't been a success, either. If the rest of her phone calls didn't turn anything up, she wasn't sure what her next step would be.

The next morning, Siena boarded the bus with the rest of the students for the Romantic Road tour. Temperatures had actually risen up into the mid-fifties, and the weather was supposed to stay mild and sunny all weekend. As the bus headed out of Munich and into the countryside, she stared at the rolling green hills and tiny farmhouses they passed along the way. The beauty of the land here made her understand why so many people had refused to leave even during terrible times.

They made several stops along the Romantic Road, first heading north to Rothenburg ob der Tauber, then coming back down south to stop for a night in Augsburg, the center of Martin Luther's Protestant Reformation. Their last stop on Sunday was Neuschwanstein Castle, one of the many castles built by King Ludwig II. The bus parked at the base of the winding path leading up the hill to the castle.

Siena was one of the first ones off the bus, along with Meg and Chen. Far above them, the castle loomed, its white turrets turning shades of yellow in the sunlight.

"It's just like Sleeping Beauty's castle." Meg smiled wistfully.

"Too bad Cody can't be here to give the princess her true love's kiss, huh?" Chen teased, playfully tugging at Meg's hair.

"Yup," Meg said. "But maybe Siena can lock Stefan up in one of those towers for a kiss of her own."

Siena followed Meg's glance to where Stefan was standing, off at a distance, snapping photos of the students with his camera. Briana must have noticed him, too, because as Siena watched, Briana pointedly sauntered right across the path of Stefan's lens. Striking a seemingly spontaneous pose, she flipped her shimmery blond hair

over her shoulder and tilted her chin to catch the sun. It was so obviously staged that Siena had to bite the inside of her cheek to keep from bursting out laughing. Stefan's reaction to Briana's performance was harder to gauge, because his camera lens hid most of his face, but after a moment, he'd redirected his lens up to the castle.

Dr. Goldstein handed out maps of the grounds and gave an overview of the history of the castle as everyone trekked up the hill. "King Ludwig the Second was known as the Swan King because of his obsession with swans as a regal symbol of beauty," she explained.

"And also known as the Mad King," Chen added as the girls pulled ahead of the rest of the group. "He was declared insane right after moving into the castle. Two days later, he went for a walk with his doctor down by Lake Starnberg, and they were both found drowned."

"Prince Charming went over the deep end?" Siena said. "Was it for the love of a woman?"

"Actually, for the love of a man, more likely," Chen said.

"Poor guy," Meg said. "All alone in the Alps with nobody to share his castle with. That's so sad."

"Trying to understand men will drive anyone crazy," Chen said. "So, Siena, stay away from the lake."

"Very funny," Siena said. "I'll figure Stefan out yet. And quit giving me bad vibes about this place. I'd like to enjoy the fairy tale, please."

And Neuschwanstein was every bit a fairy-tale castle. The hundred and seventy steps up the steep hill to the castle were worth it. Once inside, Siena couldn't stop staring at the lavish wood carvings and murals in every room. Each one depicted scenes of medieval romance—knights rescuing princesses, jousting, or even battling dragons. Siena's Moe the Knight would have fit in perfectly here. And, even though it was built in the late 1860s, the old castle had a central-air/heating system, flushing toilets, and telephones.

Siena pulled out her camcorder, breaking away from Meg and Chen for a few minutes to get some shots. She got so caught up in filming the colorful paintings and richness of the rooms, she nearly dropped the camera in surprise when Stefan tapped her on the shoulder.

"There's another place here that you might enjoy filming," he said. "The Marienbrücke, a bridge a short hike from here, has the best view of the castle. It's a very pretty walk down a wooded path. I was going to go take some photos, if you'd like to come along."

"Sounds great!" Siena smiled as they stepped outside. "I'd love to take a walk. I feel like I've been hibernating in this cold weather lately."

Stefan grinned, then nodded toward Meg and Chen, who were sitting along the castle wall. "Would they want to join us?"

When Siena asked, Meg said, using a pathetically fake tired voice, "Oh no, I don't feel like going. I'm wiped out from the walk up the hill before."

"Me, too," Chen said, stifling an even faker yawn.

"Okay, see you back at the bus," Siena said, then whispered, "And for the record, you're both horrific liars."

"Have fun with the prince," Meg whispered with a giggle.

Siena rolled her eyes, but she had to admit that she liked the idea of spending a little time alone with Stefan. Of course, as soon as that thought flitted across her mind and she and Stefan started down the path together, Briana came running up.

"I'd love to see the view from the bridge," she said, peering at Stefan through well-crimped lashes. "Can I tag along?"

"Of course," Stefan said with a smile.

Was Siena imagining things, or was that a look of genuine enthusiasm on Stefan's face? Maybe he'd just invited Siena along out of politeness, when he'd really wanted *Briana* to join him. She paused, for a second thinking she'd back out of the whole thing. But she really *did* want to see the view from the bridge, and not because Stefan had asked her, either. Why should she let her overactive imagination ruin this? That would be stupid. She needed to get herself into a more Zen mind-set. She was here to enjoy herself, with or without Stefan's one-on-one attention.

"I'm going to walk up ahead for a little bit," she said. "I want to do some filming."

She thought she saw disappointment cross Stefan's face fleetingly, but she quickly chalked that up to a trick of the eye and pulled ahead of them. She was glad she did, because the peaceful quiet of the trail was wonderful. The air was clean and crisp, and the snow-covered Alps towered over the pine trees. Reaching the bridge, she saw a waterfall cascading down below her, and the castle practically glowed golden in the sunlight. A twig snapped behind her, and she turned to see Stefan rounding the corner of the path, alone.

"Where's Briana?" Siena asked.

"She stopped to get a rock out of her shoe," he said. "One of the perils of the wilderness."

Siena smiled and started filming again with her camcorder. She could hear Stefan's camera clicking away, too.

"You're always taking pictures," she said to him as she finally put her own camera away.

"And you're always filming," he said.

"That's because I have to for class," she said. "What's your excuse?"

"I'm taking pictures of all the program students to put together photo albums for everyone," he said. "But more than that, I love *Fotografie*. After I finish at the university, I want to be a *Fotograf*."

"I think you might mean photographer?" Siena asked with a giggle.

"Yes," Stefan said. "I love looking through a lens, never knowing what I'll find."

She shrugged. "It's just what you see in front of you."

Stefan shook his head. "No, it's more. It's a story. The lens always gives you a different perspective."

She leaned against the bridge railing and closed her eyes, listening to the river running through the gorge below. When she opened them again, she noticed that Stefan had his camera pointed at her. The second their eyes met, he turned back toward the castle. She thought a flush crept across his face as he did.

"I should get back," he said suddenly. "I need to make sure Briana's all right. I'll see you at the bus?"

"Okay." She gave him the best good-natured smile she could muster. Then she muttered to herself once he was out of earshot, "She might need help with that rock."

Siena made it back it to the bus just before it left to take everyone into the tiny Bavarian town of Füssen for dinner. She'd lost track of time at the Marienbrücke and had had to scramble to make it down the hill. Of course, there was no sign of Stefan or Briana anywhere. A brief vision of the two of them snuggled up under a pine tree off the path had flashed across her mind, but she quickly shook it off. This was ridiculous, especially since she saw both of them, now, sitting in separate seats, as she boarded the bus.

Stefan gave her a smile as she passed him in the aisle, and she returned it, and then immediately scolded herself for getting her hopes up whenever he looked her way. Every time she thought she caught a hint of something more than friendship showing on his face, she'd convince herself that he was giving identical looks to Briana. Was it just his way of being nice? She couldn't really fault him for that. He was doing his *job* nearly perfectly, darn him. That's what really killed her. He seemed to be too good to mis-behave. Or maybe, *she* wasn't the girl he wanted to mis-behave with.

In Füssen, she wandered through the streets with Meg and Chen, popping in and out of little shops. Every once in a while, she noticed Stefan looking her way, but he stuck with the other resident advisers.

As the girls sat down to eat dinner, Siena spilled out her frustration about Stefan.

"I have to stop reading too much into his behavior. It's driving me nuts," she vented. "And as for Briana, in a past life, that girl was a snake."

"And how has that changed in this life?" Chen said.

"Seriously, I'm done letting Stefan get to me," she said. "We'll stay friends and that's it. I can handle it. I just need to refocus...find my inner peace."

Meg and Chen exchanged knowing glances.

"What?" Siena asked.

"Um, Siena," Meg said, "I'm not sure 'inner peace' applies when it comes to guys. Before Cody and I were going out and I didn't know where I stood with him, I was a total basket case."

Chen chimed in, "All I know is that pent-up frustration can do damage. Look what happened to King Ludwig."

"Very funny," Siena said. "Whether or not you two believe me, I am so done with him. No more drama."

"Good," Chen said with finality. "Now maybe you can focus on more important things…like passing your German test next week."

The bus unloaded a weary, travel-worn crowd back at the Lebenhaus on Sunday night. After the day she'd had, Siena was ready to catch some z's. She logged on quickly to see the latest e-mail from Lizzie, this one offering lots of advice on how she could get away with a secret fling with Stefan, and one from Foster that made her jaw drop.

To: sagittarigurl@email.com
From: fossybear@email.com
Subject: Our little secret

Senni,

Looks like I might be sticking to my end of our bargain after all. I asked someone out. (Close your mouth before something flies into it.) I prefer to leave the lucky lady anonymous for now, just in case she dumps me after our first date. Call it a protective measure for my fragile male ego. Ha. Wish me luck.

    Foss

She couldn't believe it! Foster was having more success dating these days than she was. It was pointless to try to get more details out of him, she knew, but she was still dying to know who the girl was. Maybe Lizzie had some clues; she'd e-mail her first thing tomorrow to find out. In the meantime, she needed to keep reminding herself not to crush on Stefan before her semester ended without even so much as a kiss from any prince.

Chapter Seven

Siena hit *rewind* for the umpteenth time, squirming to get comfortable in the so-called lounge chair. She was in the Film and Photography Center on campus, trying to watch some German film called *In den Tag hinein* for her film class. "Trying" was the operative word.

She had started watching it with Ansel, the cinemartist whom she'd slowly befriended, and a couple of other students from their class yesterday. Ansel explained that the English title for the film was *The Days in Between*.

"I think you'll enjoy it," he'd told her. "It's about an

impulsive young girl who just takes whatever each day may bring."

"Sounds like my kindred spirit," Siena had joked, feeling mildly enthusiastic about giving the film a shot. But she'd called it quits after a half an hour, deciding that it was better to leave willingly than to have Ansel threatening her life if she asked him to rewind one more time. To his credit, he'd been a good sport up until about the tenth time he'd rewound so that she could try to understand the fast-paced German. After that, he said he wouldn't be responsible for his actions…and it was time for her exit strategy.

Today, she'd checked out a copy of the movie from the library, and here she was, suffering in the film lab by herself. After two hours, she was still only forty minutes into it. One more time, and then she was giving up and going for a Kaffee with Meg and Chen. She hit *play* just as the door to the lab swung open. In walked Stefan, toting his camera equipment with him. Great. Getting through this film just went from improbable to impossible. She'd told Meg just last night that she'd stuck to her word for over a week, playing it cool with Stefan and focusing on classes and on her search for Peter Schwalm instead. Now all those promises she'd made to herself were as good as gone.

"Hi," she said.

"Hello," he said with a smile.

She tried to make casual conversation, explaining that

she was watching the movie for class, yada, yada. She did her best not to get flustered, but every time she looked up at Stefan's baby blue eyes, her heart stopped short.

"How is it?" Stefan asked, nodding toward the TV.

"Oh, it's great!" she lied, struggling with something, anything else, to say. "The part where the girl wins the horse race is really cool."

Well, there was a girl in the movie. That much she did know. And she thought she'd heard Ansel say something about a horse yesterday, too. Or maybe he'd said "house"? Stefan had probably never seen this movie anyway, so what did it matter?

"So," she forged on, "what are you doing here?"

Stefan held up his camera equipment. "I was planning to develop some of the photos I've taken for the program. There's a *Dunkelkammer* here as well."

"Oh, do you mean a darkroom?" she guessed. "That's the English word for it. I've never seen photos developed before."

"Well, then you definitely have to come along," Stefan said, giving her a disarmingly cute smile.

Oh no, this was not good. He was asking her to hang out with him…alone…in a tiny little room…that was dark, and quiet, and locked from the inside. This was a very bad idea.

"I should really finish this movie," Siena said. "I have to write a report about it for class by Monday."

"You can finish it later," Stefan said. "Besides, you're not really watching it."

"Yes, I am," she said defensively.

Stefan leaned toward her and whispered, "No, you're not. Because if you were, you'd know that there is no horse at all."

Siena blushed. He was right, of course, and now she had no chance of making any progress with the stupid movie—not with Stefan standing there, looking all artsy with his camera. She was such a sucker for an artist.

"Okay," she said, "But only for a few minutes."

An hour later, she was watching as Stefan filled tubs with different chemicals for developing. They had been working side by side, and Siena had even helped with some of the black-and-white prints. She'd developed one of Neuschwanstein on eight-by-ten paper that she planned to hang behind Moe the Knight at Sweet Sara's once she got home. Just watching Stefan work was enough to make her want to kiss him. He was so focused, but he always explained each step of the process to her, no matter how careful he had to be with timing everything just right.

"There's one more print I want to develop before we go," Stefan said. Using a photo enlarger, he projected an image from negative onto paper.

"Why don't you give this one a try?" he said, handing the paper to Siena.

Siena put the paper into the developer tray.

"Now put your hands on either side of the tray," Stefan said, standing beside her. When she'd done that, he gently placed his hand over hers, carefully sliding the tray back and forth. "Like that." He lifted his hand, and she let out her breath.

She focused on the picture forming on the paper, trying to cool the tingling in the tips of her fingers where his hand had been. Soon, an image slowly began to appear of a girl's face in profile, staring intently off into the distance with a little half smile on her face.

"Wow," she said. "It's beautiful."

Stefan put a hand briefly on her shoulder and whispered, "It's you."

Her heart flopped as she looked more closely at the photo. It was still hard to make out, but now she recognized her face.

He looked at her intently for a moment, then dipped the print into another tray that he called a "stop bath." "I took it when you were standing on the Marienbrücke back at the castle."

"Why?" Siena asked, holding her breath. Part of her just wanted to hear him say how he felt about her, even if it was all a figment of her poor, infatuated imagination. He'd practically been holding her hand less than five minutes ago. That had to mean something.

Stefan shrugged and stepped back, and she could

almost feel him shifting back into RA mode. "I take pictures of all the students in the program."

She nodded, turning away to hide her disappointment. She could've sworn they'd had a "moment" going on, and now he'd screwed it all up with his "I treat you the same as everyone else" b.s.

"I have to get going," Siena said, grabbing her bag off the counter. She needed to leave before she completely lost it. "I'm meeting Meg and Chen in the park."

"Okay." Stefan flipped on the overhead light, but kept his eyes focused on the prints he was hanging up to dry. "I'll see you later."

She met up with Meg and Chen in the Englischer Garten, and after Meg took one look at her face and asked her what was wrong, Siena dove into a rehash of the whole afternoon.

"He wouldn't even look at you when you left?" Meg asked as they lay in the green grass, which had finally started to sprout.

"No," Siena said. "And before that, it was like he was about to kiss me or something. He was definitely leaning in for a minute."

"Leaning is good," Meg said.

"Not when there's no follow-through." Siena sighed. "I'm getting totally mixed signals from him."

"Maybe he just can't help himself." Meg giggled.

"I think he's playing it safe and smart," Chen said, looking up from her latest page of verse. "He could get fired if he gets caught dating a student in secret."

"I know, I know. But I don't think *he's* even sure what he wants," Siena said. "What if he's okay with risking his job, but he just doesn't want to risk it for *me*?"

"Meaning?" Chen asked.

"Briana," she answered. "What if she's the one he's really interested in?"

"Then how do you explain him spending today with you?" Chen asked.

"He's spends time with her, too," Siena said. "At the Residenz and at Neuschwanstein. Once, I even saw him eating with all the Briana groupies in the cafeteria."

"He'd never go for her over you," Meg said. "I've seen the way he smiles at you. It's different."

"I don't know."

Meg giggled. "You could always tell him that you like him, and then you'd know for sure. You're the one who said you love a challenge."

Siena just stared at her. "Did *you* tell Cody you liked him before he asked you out?"

Meg blushed. "Are you kidding? I would never."

"And you're telling me to?"

"You're the carpe diem girl, not me," Meg said. "Come on, the worst that could happen is he'll say he just wants to be friends. In which case, you can move on."

"Or I could die of humiliation," Siena said.

"You believe in reincarnation, so that's no excuse," Chen joked.

"I can't do it!" Siena groaned and flopped back on the grass. "I'm living a lie. I'm really not cut out for this carpe diem stuff."

"This is exactly why I don't date," Chen said. "It makes otherwise rational people act completely crazy. Do you know they're trying to isolate the chemical in the brain that causes this imbalance? It's really not healthy."

"You'll change your mantra someday," Siena said with a laugh. "All it takes is the right guy."

"In the meantime, here on planet Earth, can I get back to my poem, please?" Chen said. "We have at least ten phone calls to make tonight from your list, and I want to finish this first."

"I know this sounds horrible, but I just can't stand the idea of another night of dead-end calls and disappointments. We need time off," Siena said. "Tonight, we should go out dancing!" She jumped up and spun a half twirl. "Where else can we go clubbing? I've only managed to go once at home, and who knows when I'll have another chance to do this."

"I don't dance," Chen said.

"You don't date. You don't dance," Siena said. "Is there anything you do do?"

"I write poems about the downfalls of civilization."

"Tonight, no poetry," Siena said. "And no love letters to Cody," she added to Meg. "Tonight, we're going to P1."

Siena decided it would not be wise to give Meg any more details about P1 than were absolutely necessary. She dressed in a sarong-style skirt and matching blue top, slipped on her bangles, then helped Meg get ready. She tied Meg's hair into a knot at the base of her neck, then pulled the ends out to form a halo of spikes around her head.

"You look stunning, dahling," she said, turning Meg around to face the mirror. "What do you think?"

Meg's cheeks reddened and she grinned. "I do look pretty, don't I?" she said shyly.

Siena tweaked her shoulder. "Need you even ask?" She ran to the closet and returned with a sequined halter in bubblegum pink. "This is the perfect match for the new 'do. Courtesy of Lizzie's packing job." The pink set off Meg's rosy cheeks even more, and the top was made to fit her petite frame. "Do you want to give it a try?"

"I don't think I should," Meg said, even though she was eyeing the halter longingly. "My parents wouldn't like me wearing it. And I don't usually wear stuff so revealing."

"Then definitely wear whatever you're comfortable with. You already look gorgeous as it is!" Siena grinned. "I just had an idea, too. We can even call Cody from the club and phone-dance with him! It'll be the first transcontinental dirty dancing ever."

Meg laughed.

"We are going to have such a blast," Siena said, playfully pulling Meg to the doorway. "Now let's go dance the night away."

By the time the girls stepped out of the cab, the line to get into P1 was three blocks long. It was then that Siena remembered what Stefan had said about P1 being pretty much impossible to get into. She would have to think fast because Meg already seemed nervous about the whole evening-out idea. And Chen, she knew without a doubt, would much rather be back in her room snuggled down with her poetry.

"All righty," she said, "all we need is a plan of action."

"I thought you had a plan before we got here," Meg said.

"Not exactly," Siena said, scanning the crowd to figure out the best way to move up in line and get past the bouncers.

"Why does that not surprise me?" Chen said, taking off her coat for the first time that night.

Siena and Meg's jaws both dropped in unison when they looked over at their friend, who was wearing a glittery mini and three-inch stilettos, ready to rock.

"What?" Chen said with a shrug.

"Chen!" Meg cried. "You look totally glam."

"And you said you don't dance," Siena said. Nothing could surprise her after this.

"I don't," Chen said. "But I never said I don't go clubbing. Occasionally." She grinned. "It's a study in human nature. For my poetry."

"Gotcha," Siena said.

"Well, since you two have yet to come up with a plan to get us into this place," Chen said, "I'll have to take matters into my own hands. Come on." She led Siena to the front of the line while Meg followed in baby steps.

Then, without even a moment's hesitation, Chen went up to the bouncer, and in perfect German nonchalantly told him her name was on his list and that she was just running late. He nodded, and Chen quickly motioned Siena and Meg to follow her into the club. They had to practically drag Meg through the door as fellow clubbers cursed them from their places in line.

But as soon as they were inside, Siena let out a triumphant whoop. "You did it, Chen! You are a goddess!"

Chen just smiled. "Remember that, girls. 'Cause you'll never see it again."

"Once was enough for a lifetime." Siena laughed.

The club was already rocking with a techno beat, calling Siena to hit the dance floor. She even convinced Meg to dance, too. Colored spotlights swung around the room,

118

and strobe lights popped nonstop. They danced until their feet throbbed and Siena's hair was matted to her neck. No matter how hard she and Meg tried, though, they couldn't get Chen out on the dance floor.

"I'm people-watching," Chen called out from the bar when they motioned for her to join them. "Don't you worry about me."

Finally, when Siena couldn't take another step, she headed for a stool at the bar. Meg was still out on the floor. There was no stopping her now that she'd found her groove. Siena ordered a water and gulped it down. Just then she spotted Ansel over in the corner, moodily sipping a drink and having an intense conversation with some of his similarly brooding friends. She waved at him, and he nodded with his normal tormented-artist frown. Suddenly she had an idea of such greatness, such brilliance, it was nothing short of a psychic epiphany. She walked over to him with the perfect plan of action. A few minutes later, she reeled in Meg and plopped down next to Chen, who'd been guarding the purses and jotting down verses on a bar napkin.

"Chen, your knight in angsty armor has arrived," Siena said.

"What's that supposed to mean?"

"It means that there's a certain guy in a certain film class of mine who wants to meet you," Siena said proudly. "He's over at the bar right now."

"You are not setting me up," Chen said. "The whole concept is medieval. Do men think we sit around just waiting for their attention?"

"Actually, he's waiting for *you* to talk to *him*," Siena said while Meg broke into laughter.

"No."

"He's fluent in three languages."

"Nope."

"His favorite poet is Heinrich Heine and his films are interpretations of his poems."

Silence.

Siena waited while Chen stared at the floor. She knew she had her when Chen said, "You can introduce me, but don't expect me to dance with him."

"Never." Siena smiled. "Didn't I mention? He's not the dancing type, either."

In the wee hours, the three girls got back to the dorm. Meg and Chen headed straight to bed, but Siena was still wired from the energy of the club. They'd had such a blast, and she was especially happy to see that her little matchmaking attempt with Chen and Ansel had been a success. She knew the two of them had a strong karmic connection, and Chen had gotten his phone number, too. "Not that I'll call him," Chen had said, but Siena knew from the small smile on her face that she would.

She put on her pj's and went down to the computer lab to check her e-mail, wanting to write to Lizzie and Foster about her awesome night, and hoping she'd be able to get some sleep afterward. Lizzie was in an instant-messaging mood and had what she thought was the perfect solution for how to deal with Stefan:

DeLizious: When in doubt, a little bit of lip service goes a long way. So plant one on him! You know you want to. . .

ZenSien: I am NOT that desperate.

DeLizious: Yes . . . you are. ☺ BTW, how's the search for Peter going?

ZenSien: Going nowhere at the moment. And I'm running out of time. Midterms are next week, and then Dr. Goldstein's taking us to Salzburg, Austria for a weekend. Chen and I only have about fifty more numbers to call, but we won't have time until after that trip.

DeLizious: You'll find him.

ZenSien: Easier said than done.

DeLizious: Don't get cynical on me now. Not your style. If anyone can track him down, Senni, you can.

ZenSien: Thnx.

DeLizious: So, I guess you've heard that Foster is no longer in need of platonic female friends. Our little boy's all growed up.

ZenSien: Does that mean you've uncovered his mystery girl?

DeLizious: Not sure yet, but I'm rooting for the cute redhead in his bio class. She's had her eye on him for months.

ZenSien: I wish he'd just tell us, the little stinker.

DeLizious: If I don't find out soon, I'll try torture. Nitynite. Don't let Stefanistic give you any love bites. Hee-hee.

Chapter Eight

Siena was proud of what a good job she'd done of avoiding alone time with Stefan since their day at the photo lab. Every once in a while, she'd see Briana search him out in the cafeteria so that she could eat with him. Even though there were always other resident advisers with them, too, Briana flirted outright. Of course, Stefan ate with lots of different students, but Siena always saw, or imagined seeing, an extra-wide smile on his face when Briana was around.

On top of that, she couldn't figure out how, with as

much time as Briana spent partying, flirting, or gabbing on her cell, the girl still managed to be at the top of the class. This Friday, everyone was getting their midterm papers back in European history, and it was no big surprise to Siena when Briana took the spotlight.

"I'd like to commend you all on a job well done," Dr. Schultz said in his typical somber tone as he passed out the papers. "However, there was one paper in particular that was truly well executed. Briana, I'd love for you to read an excerpt from your paper while I hand out the rest of the midterms."

"He's got to be kidding," Chrissy whispered to Siena.

"Nope. She's unbeatable," Siena replied.

Briana blushed, hesitated long enough to seem appropriately humble, and then began reading. Even though Siena hated to admit it, she was impressed by Briana's writing. It was fluid and clear, with an academic-sounding vocab word thrown in here and there.

"It is a good paper," she said to Chrissy and Mia as class was ending.

"Yeah, but how could she have written a paper like that?" Mia said. "All she ever does in class is pass notes to Stacy."

There was something about Briana's perfect paper that bugged Siena, too, but she couldn't put her finger on exactly what. It was probably just Briana's gloating over the whole thing. She didn't have long to think about it, though, because soon Dr. Schultz was at Siena's desk with her paper.

"Much, much better." He smiled at her, and she was thrilled to see the *A* at the top of her essay.

"That's great," Chrissy said when she saw it. "Another analysis of maypoles?"

"Not exactly," Siena confessed. "I stuck with a tried-and-true topic this time: Battle of the Bulge. Not creative, but I guess A-worthy."

She packed her bag and left class with Chrissy and Mia. "I'll see you guys tomorrow on the ski trip, right?"

"Definitely," Mia said.

Siena couldn't wait for the "study-free" weekend of sightseeing and skiing around Salzburg, Austria. Salzburg was only a few hours away from Munich, and she was psyched to be seeing another country. She couldn't wait to give skiing a try, too. It would be a much-needed break after finishing midterms. She still hadn't made any headway with Peter Schwalm, and she wanted one weekend without worrying about it.

By the time her German film class was ending, all she could think about was getting R & R. But first, she had to get through presenting Dr. Nielson with the work she'd done so far on her film piece for the German experience. It was a collage of DVD clips she'd compiled of everything

she'd seen in Germany so far—Neuschwanstein Castle, the interior of St. Peter's Church, and more.

"These are all nice shots, Siena," Dr. Nielson said afterward. "But I can't help feeling that it's missing something essential to successful cinematography."

Siena racked her brain, thinking of what she might have done wrong. She'd finally gotten her footing in history, and now she was losing ground in film. Wasn't this just the way the tea leaves tumbled? "I set up the composition like you showed me," she explained, "and the lighting. I'm not sure what else to do."

"There's nothing wrong with the film," Dr. Nielson said, readjusting his blue glasses. "But it doesn't give me any sense of emotion. These are all beautiful places, but where is the story? What do they *mean* to you?"

Siena stared at the now blank screen, completely at a loss for words. She didn't have answers to any of those questions.

Dr. Nielson handed her the DVD and patted her on the shoulder. "Give it some thought. There's probably much more to your connection to this country than what you've shown me here."

He left the classroom, and Siena's head sank down to the tabletop. Ansel, who'd been waiting for her since the end of class, sat down in the desk next to hers. They'd been planning to meet up with Chen and Meg at Café-

Konditorei Schneller. Now Siena wasn't in any kind of mood for socializing, although before she'd been dying to catch a glimpse of Chen and Ansel flirting. She was tempted to head back to the dorm for an aromatherapy session, but even that might not lift her spirits at this point.

"That was harsh!" she cried, thinking again about Dr. Nielson's comments.

"Not really," Ansel said. "Just truthful. Every artist needs brutal honesty to rise above mediocrity. Put the DVD in again. Let's process."

She'd noticed that *process* was Ansel's favorite word for deep, gut-wrenching critique sessions—the kind he thought were a necessary anguish of any good filmmaker.

As she watched the film a second time through, she saw what Dr. Nielson was talking about.

"He's right," she said afterward. "It's nothing but a lot of pretty pictures."

"It makes a great tourism video," Ansel said. "But it's not art until your blood oozes out of it."

Not the most tactful way of putting it, but she knew he had a point. There was no sense of how Germany had changed her, touched her heart. She'd been trying so hard to play by the rules in her classes after her disastrous maypole essay, she hadn't taken any risks at all with this film, which was *supposed* to be "experimental"!

She stood up, stuffing the DVD she'd made so

painstakingly into her bag. "Let's go. I want to stop at the post office on the way to the café."

"Why?"

"To mail this off to my mom," she said. "She and my friends can watch it to see all the cool places I've been. At least *they'll* get some use out of it."

She'd start over from scratch and make a new film for the German experience project. She didn't have a clue what it would be about, but she knew she'd better figure it out, and fast.

When she got back to the dorm later that night, she stopped to check her e-mail. After weeks of hearing nothing, finally she'd gotten an e-mail from Anna Schlegel! She opened it, her heart racing. It was written in German, but to her delight, she could actually understand it! For once, she didn't need Chen to help her translate. After a month and a half in Germany, she was finally starting to get it.

In the e-mail, Anna apologized for not being in touch sooner, but she'd been on vacation and had only just gotten back home and heard the message. She was delighted to hear that Siena was in town, and she wanted to meet her for dinner on the following Monday at a Munich restaurant called Dreigroschenkeller.

Siena pulled out her German/English dictionary and wrote an e-mail back saying she'd love to meet her and mentioning her search for Peter Schwalm, too (as best as she could in German, anyway). After she signed off, she ran upstairs to tell Meg and Chen what happened. Maybe this was it—maybe Anna would have some of the information she was looking for. Even if her love life was a total lost cause, finishing her dad's list didn't have to be.

Chapter Nine

Siena had never seen this much snow in her life. The group had left Munich long before dawn, and after a Eurorail ride (her very first ever!), they'd arrived in Salzburg. The landscape of Austria didn't look so different from Germany, but Salzburg was a much smaller, quainter town than Munich, with cobblestone alleyways and tiny curio shops and cafés everywhere. And who could forget its real claim to fame? As Meg had reminded her in an obvious state of Julie Andrews–induced euphoria, Salzburg had once been home to the von Trapp family of *The Sound of Music* fame. Siena had no doubt she'd get a large dose of "Do-Re-Mi" tomorrow, since Meg had made her and Chen swear to take the four-hour, all-inclusive, panoramic *The Sound of Music* tour.

Today, though, she hadn't had time to explore the town, since as soon as the group had arrived, they split into those who were going skiing and those who weren't. She'd boarded the snow shuttle that took her, along with Meg, Mia, Chrissy, and about fifteen other students, high into the Alps for skiing.

Here, the mountain peaks of the Bad Gastein ski resort surrounded her in blankets of white. It was the end of March, and a springtime sun shone down, making the snow glisten. It was like being in the middle of a huge snow globe, and just as pretty. When she was little, she'd made a few trips up to Big Bear Mountain with her mom to see snow, but that mountain was more like a molehill in comparison to this.

"These things weigh a ton," she grunted to Meg as she forced her feet into an unbelievably tight pair of rented ski boots.

"They're supposed to keep you from falling," Meg said, already strapped into hers.

Siena boarded the lift with Meg, Chrissy, and Mia. It was a good thing the weather was warm, at least, considering the jeans and light city jackets she and Meg were making do with. But as her toes went numb inside her boots, she started to wish she'd followed Chen's example

and sat this one out. Chen had opted out of skiing, excusing herself by saying she wanted to visit Mozart's birthplace in Salzburg instead. Siena and Meg both knew the real reason she wasn't here. Ansel had driven to Salzburg separately and met up with her this morning. The two of them were attending an independent film festival in town. Chen wouldn't admit it, but Siena knew that the girl had it ... bad. She'd even been forgetting to get on Siena's case about her German lessons. If Chen was getting a soft side, there had to be some love going on.

"All right, ladies," Siena said, feeling brave once she'd successfully deboarded the lift with all limbs intact. "Let's be one with nature. Just point me downhill."

"Siena, you and Meg might want to try a beginner slope first," Mia suggested, studying her trail map. "This run is for intermediate skiers."

"I'm a ski-by-the-seat-of-my-pants kind of girl," Siena said. She pointed to the smooth snow. "Meg and I can definitely handle that."

"Um, I'd really like to get back to Texas in one piece." Meg peered uncertainly at the hill.

"Since when are you a pessimist?" Siena laughed. "Let's go!" She scooted to the edge of the slope and leaped off.

The first five seconds were thrilling. Then her skis crossed and she ate a mouthful of powder. "I'm all right!" she called back to the girls with a laugh. But she soon discovered that jeans didn't hold up too well after, oh, say, the thirtieth time she face-planted into the snow. Meg, on the other hand, had actually gotten the hang of skiing once she stopped being petrified. She was waiting halfway down the hill, grinning, when Siena finally half tumbled, half slid to a stop beside her.

"This is not quite the revitalizing experience I'd imagined," Siena said as she started downhill again. And those were her famous last words before the tree came out of nowhere. The next thing she knew, her skis were pointing skyward, wrapped around the thankfully small evergreen, and she was stuck.

"Are you at one with nature now?" Chrissy cried between bouts of hysterical laughter. Meg and Mia couldn't say anything, seeing as they were doubled over laughing, too.

"Um, a little help?" Siena said. She was trying to untangle herself in between her own giggling fits when, out of the corner of her eye, she saw a red jacket making its way toward her.

"Did someone say 'help'?" Stefan said as he slid to a stop and inspected her dilemma. Even in her semifrozen state, Siena noticed how the red in his jacket set off his blond curls. God, if he looked good holding a camera, he . looked even better on skis.

"Ah, my rescuer has arrived," she said.

"Not just yet," Stefan said playfully. "It's not every day I cross paths with an abominable snow girl." He pulled his camera out of his jacket, and Siena watched helplessly as he snapped a few pictures.

Once Stefan had finally dug her out, the first thing she did was fire a well-packed snowball his way. An all-out war ensued, with Siena reigning victorious after tackling him and giving him a faceful of snow. Finally, both snow-covered and laughing, they rejoined the rest of the group, and Stefan soon said good-bye to go help organize lunch for the students.

"I don't know whether y'all are going to end up kissing or killing each other," Meg said to Siena, rolling her eyes. "But I do know you're never going to make it to the end of the semester without one of the two."

"Maybe both," Siena said, right before she belly flopped into the snow.

"I think I'll stick to yoga from now on," Siena muttered as she eased herself into a seat on *The Sound of Music* bus the next morning.

"Skiing didn't agree with you, huh?" Chen teased, herself looking like she was in an unusually cheery mood. Siena could only guess that Ansel was responsible. She was pretty sure that the prospect of spending the entire morning singing along with Julie Andrews wouldn't put a smile like that on Chen's face.

"It wasn't the skiing. The skiing was great. It was the falling," Siena said, checking out another purple bruise on her arm that had blossomed overnight.

Still, even though it hurt to laugh, she couldn't help it when she looked over at Meg, who was practically bouncing out of her seat with excitement. Meg was already flipping through her *Sound of Music* keepsake album, even though the bus was just pulling away from the curb. "I'm so glad y'all came with me," she said, her eyes aglow with Maria mania. "I've watched this movie about a hundred times. I know all the words and everything."

The overture to the movie welled up over the bus's speakers, and Mike the Tour Guide clapped his hands. "Who's ready for four hours of fun?" he called enthusiastically. Everyone whooped and hollered. "I expect all of you to sing along with Maria. The louder the better."

Chen groaned. "Two minutes of 'The Sound of Muzak' and I already have a headache."

"Oh, come on, get into the spirit," Siena said. "Bursting into song is very therapeutic. Just look at Maria. She was a totally self-actualized person."

"Are you kidding?" Chen said. "She had the worst taste I've ever seen. Nobody gets away with making clothes from curtains unless they're Versace. Plus, she married a father figure. A classic example of an Elektra complex. What kind of self-respecting woman marries a whistle-toting, conceited chauvinist?"

"The Captain was a changed man after he met Maria," Meg said with total seriousness.

"And so good-looking, too." Siena winked at Chen. "And what about your newest 'favorite thing'? I know you're dying to sing about him. You could try 'High on a Hill Lived a Lonely Goatee.' Or how about 'Anselweiss'?"

"You're killing me," Chen said, but she was smiling.

Siena threw her arms around Meg and the two of them burst into an ear-bending rendition of "The Hills Are Alive."

"Our first stop on the tour is Leopoldskron Castle," Guide Mike said. "Here Maria and the von Trapp children took their famous dip in the lake. But little Gretl couldn't swim. When the scene was shot, Gretl drank 'half the lake' before one of the crew jumped in to rescue her."

"That was one of my favorite scenes!" Meg beamed, madly snapping pictures.

Later, when the bus stopped at the gazebo setting for the infamous "Sixteen Going on Seventeen" song, Siena saw Meg's enthusiasm reach heights that could only be replicated by the great Julie Andrews herself.

"I dreamed that my first kiss would be in a gazebo," she said.

"And was it?" Siena asked.

Meg blushed. "It was under the Caldwell water tower. Cody looked all over for a gazebo, but there weren't any in our town, so he said the next best thing would have to do."

Chen shook her head, reading deadpan from the lyrics.

"'Fellows you meet may tell you you're sweet, and willingly you believe.'"

"Aha!" Meg said. "I *knew* you were a closet *Sound of Music* junkie! Come out…set yourself free."

For the next few hours, the bus wound through the outskirts of Salzburg, where they saw Maria's abbey and Mirabell Gardens, where "Do-Re-Mi" was sung. Then out into the Salzkammergut Lake District they went, to the tiny town of Mondsee, which held the cathedral where Maria and the Captain were married and "the best" strudel in all of Austria was made. By the time they finished the tour, Meg looked like she'd died and gone to Rodgers and Hammerstein Heaven, and Siena had even gotten Chen to give in and sing along to a few songs.

She boarded the train to Munich feeling refreshed after her weekend free of school worries, boy worries, and Peter Schwalm worries. Snarfing creamed apple strudel and cheesily humming "I Have Confidence" with two good friends—life abroad couldn't get much better than that. At least for now. She had tomorrow to deal with everything else.

Tomorrow came all too soon. Siena rushed back to the dorm after class on Monday just in time to change for her dinner with Anna Schlegel. She tried not to be nervous, but meeting a member of her dad's family for the first time was a huge deal. What if Anna didn't like her? What if *she* didn't

like Anna? So many questions filled her mind as she hurried to the restaurant.

The second she stepped through the doors of Dreigroschenkeller, her worries vanished. If Anna could pick such a cool place for their first meeting, she had to be pretty cool herself. The restaurant was more of a cellar, partially underground, dimly lit and full of nooks and crannies that overflowed with fun knickknacks. She was still studying every detail of the place when a woman who had to be Anna walked through the door. Siena recognized her immediately. Even though they were cousins and not siblings, Anna actually resembled her dad, at least from what she could tell from old photos of him. She was younger than he would have been now, with a cheerful smile and welcoming face.

Siena gave Anna a wave and a smile just before Anna enveloped her in a hug.

Once they had made their way to a quieter table in the corner, Anna sat back, beaming at Siena.

"I love this place," Siena started in halting German, motioning to the walls of knickknacks surrounding them.

"It's one of my favorite spots in München," Anna said, speaking German slowly for Siena's sake. "It's named after *The Threepenny Opera* by Kurt Weill and Bertolt Brecht." She hummed a few notes that Siena vaguely recognized. "Each of these rooms is made to look like a part of the story. The jail, the wedding room, even the brothel."

"Fun!" Siena said as they ordered their food. "I'd love to bring my friends back here sometime. This is really off the beaten path…perfect for us." She struggled momentarily with her German, but Anna was patient with her. If she talked slowly, Anna seemed to understand almost everything she said.

"You look like your father when he was younger," Anna said. "One summer when we were teenagers, I came to America to visit him. I was shy back then, but Bill was so outgoing. He told me once he wanted to backpack around the world. He would be proud of you for making this trip."

"You think so?" Siena said.

"As much of an adventurer as he was?" Anna smiled. "Of course. And I think it would make him happy to know that you're trying to find Peter. But I'm not sure how much of a help I can be in your search."

As they ate, Anna told Siena that her family had been lucky enough to be living in West Germany before the Berlin Wall went up, so she never had to fight for her freedom the way Siena's dad had.

"My mother, too, tried to contact Peter. Your grandfather George begged her to after he reached America. But we had no more luck than he did," Anna told her. "The Wall cut off a lot of communication. By the time contact between east and west was permitted again, we couldn't find Peter."

"Oh, I see," Siena said, trying not to let this discourage her too much.

Anna gave Siena's hand a reassuring pat. "I do have one thing that might be of some help, though." She pulled a piece of paper from her purse and gave it to Siena. "These are addresses from years ago. Both were Berlin apartments Peter lived in right after he helped your family escape. You might be able to find phone numbers, or maybe speak to someone in the buildings."

Siena studied the addresses, hoping beyond hope that one of them might finally lead somewhere.

"And one more thing," Anna said, handing an envelope to Siena. "This...is for you."

Siena pulled a photograph out of the envelope. A little boy stared out of the picture, standing next to a young man and woman. They were all smiling happily at the camera. The Statue of Liberty was just barely visible in the faded background behind them.

"That is your father and your grandparents," Anna said. "It was taken right after they arrived in America. Your grandfather mailed it to my mother. He tried to convince my parents to come to America, too, but they would never leave their farm here."

Siena carefully put the photograph back inside the envelope for safekeeping, feeling like she was the new guardian of a rare treasure. "Wow. Thank you," she said, so grateful to this woman who had already helped her so much.

"Enough of the past for now," Anna said with a smile. "I

want to hear all about you. It's not every day I get to visit with my second cousin from America."

After hours of talking with Anna, Siena came back to the Lebenhaus with a grin glued to her face. She and Anna had had such a great time together.

"Next time you visit Germany," Anna had told her as they said good night, "you will stay with me. My door will always be open for you." Siena had no doubt the invitation was heartfelt.

Once she gave Chen and Meg a rundown of the whole night, she showed them the addresses she'd gotten from Anna.

"If the apartment buildings are still standing, we should be able to get some phone numbers. We'll look them up on the Internet. I've got a huge bio project to work on this week, and we've got the program trip to Dachau next Saturday, but right after that," Chen said.

Afterward, Siena tried to sleep, but every detail of her visit with Anna kept running through her mind. Something good—no, *great*—had happened today. Even if she wasn't able to find Peter, at least she'd gotten the chance to meet Anna. In some strange way, seeing Anna and hearing the stories she told about her dad's family had made her feel closer to her dad. She'd always be grateful for that, no matter what happened with the rest of her semester here.

Chapter Ten

When Siena boarded the S-Bahn train for the program's day trip to Dachau, the first concentration camp created in Germany during World War II, the sun was shining brightly and the air was really, truly warm for the first time since she'd arrived. But during the bus ride from the train station to Dachau, the whole group seemed to forget about the beautiful spring day and slowly grew silent. The stark camp stood behind a high wire fence. Just looking at it made a chill run through Siena. She studied the sign at one of the entrances that read ARBIT MACHT FREI.

"Work makes one free," she translated slowly, then

cringed. "I can't believe that prisoners were actually told that. Working day and night without enough food or sleep. For what—the smallest chance at freedom?"

"It's disgusting," Meg whispered, "especially when most of the people who walked through those gates never walked out."

"Hypocrisy makes a great blindfold," Chen said, staring at the sign.

They walked past a memorial built to the victims of Dachau—an abstract metal sculpture depicting people caught in barbed wire. Siena filmed some of what she saw as she explored the grounds, but she couldn't bring herself to put it all on camera. It just didn't seem right.

Most of the barracks where the prisoners slept were gone, but there was one that had been rebuilt. She stared in at the tiny little bunks and communal toilets in the small, cramped quarters.

"I'm not sure I'll ever understand people's cruelty to one another," Chen said.

"But for every act of cruelty is one of great kindness," Siena said. "There were lives that were saved, and amazing people risked their lives to rescue others. That's the balance I try to see in the universe, anyway."

As they approached the crematorium, Meg whispered, "Everything looks so gray."

Even though the sky was only partly cloudy, Siena saw exactly what she meant. The whole place felt dark and

barren, like a shadow was stretched over the camp. The crunching of the gravel under their feet was the only sound they heard when they came to the crematorium doorway. Dr. Goldstein had told them that Dachau never had a gas chamber, but there were a number of medical experiments performed on prisoners that resulted in death, as well as thousands of executions.

Siena hesitated at the doorway. She dreaded looking inside, but knew she had to. Finally, she stepped through. Large brick ovens were lined up neatly one after another, big enough to hold...her stomach suddenly lurched. She rushed outside, gulping in the fresh air as tears filled her eyes. Taking a seat on the nearest bench, she struggled to calm her nerves.

A warm arm slipped around her, and she found herself looking into Stefan's concerned face.

"Are you all right?" he asked, keeping a firm, steady hold on her.

Siena wiped at her eyes and inhaled a deep breath, for a minute letting herself lean against him. "I just needed some air. It's all so horrible."

Stefan nodded. "It's a difficult place to visit. Bringing students here is a part of my job that I hate."

"I don't blame you," she said. "Seeing it once is all I could handle."

He seemed to want to stay there with her to make sure

she was all right, but then other students emerged from the crematorium, Briana among them. Briana was staring directly at them, and once Stefan saw that, he immediately pulled away and stood up.

Siena stared at him, more confused than ever. Was it his job he was worried about, or was it Briana's sudden appearance? At that moment, she wished they could at least have a normal friendship, if nothing more. But how could they even be friends if being with her one-on-one in front of everyone else made him so uncomfortable? The times when she'd seen him and Briana together, he never seemed this nervous. Did that mean he liked Briana so much that he didn't care what everyone else thought? Or did it mean that he *didn't* like Briana, so he wasn't so self-conscious about being around her?

"Why don't I see if I can find you some tissues?" Stefan offered, awkwardly glancing back and forth between her and the other students. Siena saw Meg and Chen stepping out of the barracks, too, looking her way.

She stood up. Maybe this was all her fault. Maybe she was the one who couldn't handle a friendship with him without always wanting something more. Regardless, she just couldn't deal right now. "Thanks," she told him, "but don't worry about it. I'm all right. I'm going to catch up with Meg and Chen."

"Siena, wait…" Stefan said, but she was already walking

away, only looking back once to see Stefan standing in the courtyard, a look of confusion on his face.

It was a gloomy ride back to the dorm. Nobody could shake the sadness of what they'd seen.

"What happened back there?" Meg asked her finally. "I saw you with Stefan, and it seemed like something was wrong."

Siena sighed. "I don't really feel like talking about it. I'm just not sure I can handle hanging around him anymore, that's all."

"If you want to talk later…" Meg started.

But she didn't. Why should she torture herself overanalyzing every glance Stefan gave her if it was going to go nowhere? It was fun being with him, but if she couldn't handle it without wanting something more, then *she* was the one who needed to readjust her thinking. Why couldn't relationships with guys *ever* be normal?

Feeling homesick for the first time since the semester had started, she checked her e-mail when she got back to the dorm. She was a little bit cheered to see e-mails from Lizzie and Foster, and Foster's was newsworthy. He had asked that redhead from his bio class to spring formal! Her name was Courtney, and according to him, she was already a huge fan of Sweet Sara's. Siena was impressed. If Foss had brought Courtney to the café, things must be getting serious. *P.S.,* he'd written. *If this Stefan doesn't realize what a fantastic girl you are, he's a total ass. ;)*

Siena dropped Foster a congratulatory e-mail, glad to see that at least *his* love life was working. She wasn't in any mood to hang out with everyone in the lounge afterward, or do yoga, so she curled up on her bed to work on her final history paper. It was a sad, sad day when she chose studying over socializing.

Chen knocked on the door a couple hours later. "Still alive in there?" she called, peeking around the door. "Meg thought you wanted some alone time, but she's downstairs worrying about you. And *you're* up here studying of your own free will? This is serious."

"I'm fine," Siena said. "It's just been a long day. Call it a bout of crappy-mood weather."

"You know, Germans have a saying. 'There is no bad weather, only bad clothes.'" Chen smiled. "Words to live by."

Siena had to laugh at that.

"I'd take you shopping at the Dolcé boutique, but I've come up with something I think you'll like better. Not that you should expect me to be the bearer of sunshine and smiles every day. That's Meg's domain. All that cheeriness would kill my poetry." Chen handed a piece of paper to Siena. "I found these on the net this afternoon. Two phone numbers from the addresses Anna gave you for Peter in Berlin."

Siena stared at the numbers. "This is it, isn't it? We fin-ished calling all the other numbers last week. What do we do if this doesn't work?"

"This one time only, I'm going to play the optimist and tell you that I have a hunch about this," Chen said. "Now don't tell me you still want to study when we have more important work to do."

Siena really smiled for the first time all day. She grabbed her calling card off her desk, with its twenty measly min-utes remaining. "Let's go."

Downstairs in the lounge, she nervously dialed the first number. If neither of these numbers led anywhere, she'd have to go back to California without finishing her dad's list.

Chen and Meg were both watching anxiously. After all the help they'd given her, they seemed just as determined to do this as she was.

A woman answered the phone on the second ring, but when Siena asked about a Peter Schwalm, the woman said she didn't remember anyone by that name. She'd been in the same apartment for twenty years, and she didn't know who had lived there before her. Siena listened with a sink-ing spirit. She thanked the woman and hung up, slowly shaking her head at Meg and Chen's expectant faces.

"Try the next one," Meg said, nibbling her nails. "It's got to be the one."

Siena took a deep breath and dialed the second number. A gruff-sounding man answered the phone. As Siena asked her questions, she found out that he was the landlord of the building.

"Peter Schwalm?" He grumbled after she had said the name. "He moved out ten years ago. But I still get his mail. So much mail. Always, I have to forward the mail to him."

"Could you give me his phone number or address, please?" she stammered as Chen and Meg scrambled frantically to scrounge up a pen.

"*Danke schön!*" she said, and hung up the phone.

"So?" Meg asked.

"I got a number!" she cried.

"Well, what are you waiting for?" Chen asked.

Siena dialed with trembling fingers. Each ring echoed in her ear almost as loudly as her pounding heart. Finally, she heard a click on the other end of the line. There was a pause, and then a husky voice, rumbling with old age, said, "*Hallo.*"

"*Hallo,*" she said in the clearest German she could muster. "May I speak to Peter Schwalm, please?"

"Speaking," the voice answered.

She gripped the phone with one hand and steadied herself against the couch with the other. The words she spoke rose out of her through a thick haze of nerves, like she was talking from the bottom of a mud puddle.

"Herr Schwalm," she said. "My name is Siena Bernstein. I think you may have known my grandparents."

"What did he say?" Meg asked as soon as Siena hung up the phone. "Was it him?"

Siena nodded, breaking into a grin so wide her cheeks hurt. "He wants to meet me next weekend," she cried.

Meg squealed and hugged her, and even Chen, after trying her best to remain her calm, collected self, finally shrugged and joined in.

"He could barely speak when I told him who I was," Siena said. "He just kept repeating the word *Wundertat* over and over again."

"It means 'miracle,'" Chen said quietly.

That made tears spring to Siena's eyes. "He sounded so happy to hear from me."

"Of course he did!" Meg cried. "You're the proof that your grandparents and your dad made it to America. It's the happy ending he never knew about until now."

"So is he coming to Munich next weekend?" Chen asked.

"No," Siena said. "He's eighty years old and can't travel much anymore." She looked at the paper where she'd written his address. "Which is why I'm going to Weinheim to see him. It's outside Heidelberg, only a couple hours from here."

She waited for what she knew was bound to come next in three, two...

"But, Siena," Meg said. "You're not supposed to be taking trips outside Munich by yourself."

And there it was.

"Remember what Dr. Goldstein said about traveling outside the program?" Meg went on. "And how would you even get there? By train?"

Siena shook her head. "He said the train doesn't go to Weinheim."

"Let me get this straight," Chen said. "You told this man that you'd meet him next Saturday in Weinheim, but you have no way to get there. And you're going to break the rules to do it. Have I taught you nothing about planning ahead?"

"It's predestined, Chen," Siena said with a smile. "I don't know how, but I'm going."

"This is Martin Luther's country, home of the Lutheran Church," Chen said. "He didn't believe in predestination."

"Yeah, yeah, so Dr. Goldstein's said. But Martin Luther never read horoscopes," Siena said. "Look, I've been playing by the rules in class, and I'm missing out on a chance with Stefan because of rules. There are times in life when you have to bend the rules. This is one of them."

"You're right," Meg piped up. "You have to go."

"And don't even think about going alone," Chen said. "I'm in."

But just the idea of breaking the rules made Meg's face turn a shade paler.

"You don't have to come," Siena told her. "I don't want you to get in trouble for going with me."

"I'm in, too." Meg sighed. "But for the record, if my parents ever find out about this, I was taken against my will."

"What, kidnapped by two of your best friends?" Chen said skeptically. "Oh, they're sure to believe that."

Meg's eyes lit up. "You're my best friends?" She beamed.

"Don't get all sentimental on me," Chen said, the start of a smile pulling at her lips. "It's just a figure of speech."

"Uh-huh." Meg laughed.

"All right, guys, help me out here," Siena said. "We need someone with a car."

They all went silent as they gave that some thought.

"Stefan," Meg and Chen suddenly said together.

Siena shook her head violently. "No way," she said. "I am not groveling for a ride from him."

A half hour of torment later, and she was groveling.

"Hi," she said when Stefan opened his door and invited her in.

"Hi," he said, looking a little relieved, but confused, to see her. "Are you all right? I wasn't sure. You seemed so upset at Dachau."

"I'm fine," she said, blushing at the memory of her earlier behavior. "I just...It was a bad day is all." She cleared her throat, brought her eyes up to meet his, and said, "I need a favor."

She explained the whole story to him, pushing past the awkwardness between them. When she was finished, she chanced a glance at his face. He stared thoughtfully at the ground for what seemed like an eternity while she contemplated all of the reasons he had *not* to help her, his job being first and foremost. Finally, he looked up at her.

"I can take next weekend off," he said, "and I have friends in Heidelberg at the university I haven't seen for a while. I'll take you."

"That would be great," Siena said, smiling gratefully.

"Just don't mention this to anyone else, all right?" he said. "You're not even supposed to be leaving Munich, and I'm definitely not supposed to be driving you."

"Sure," Siena said. "Meg and Chen are coming, too, but none of us will say a word. I know you could get into major trouble."

"Good. Well, I'll see you later," he said.

"Hey," she said quietly, causing him to freeze in the doorway. "Thank you."

He opened his mouth like he wanted to say something, then closed it again. He finally sighed and gave her a small smile. "*Bitte sehr*. You're welcome," he said, and shut the door.

As Siena turned away, she smacked right into Briana,

making her drop an armful of books and papers all over the floor of the hallway.

"Don't you ever watch where you're going?" Briana snapped, all the while looking from Stefan's room to Siena and back again.

"I'm sorry," Siena said, and meant it. This was no time for petty catfights; she had other things to worry about.

She bent down to help, but Briana hurriedly scrambled to pick up the papers before she could touch them.

"Just leave them," Briana said, sighing dramatically. Siena saw that they were photocopies of pages, probably from the library books Briana had under her arms. She caught some of the book titles; they all had to do with the history of Germany.

"I'll help," she offered one more time.

"Never mind," Briana said. "Really, it's fine." She actually looked a little flustered herself.

"Okay!" Siena shrugged. As she walked away, she tried to forget that she had run into Briana, but her gut told her that it meant one thing—trouble.

Chapter Eleven

As Stefan maneuvered his car onto a narrow road along a quiet river, Siena glanced up from the map and caught her breath. A collage of red-roofed buildings nestled cozily against a lush green hillside. Set high on the hill overlooking the town were the beautiful ruins of a sand-colored castle.

"Is this it?" she asked.

Stefan nodded with a smile. "*Willkommen in Heidelberg.* This is the Neckar River we're driving along. It runs right through the city. The university is over there." He pointed to some industrial-style modern buildings mixed in with a

few antiquated ones set farther back behind the riverfront. "And up there"—he pointed to the castle standing guard over the city—"is Heidelberg Schloss."

"You're a miracle worker, Stefan," Chen said from the backseat. "If you hadn't double-checked Siena on that turn off the autobahn, we'd be in Switzerland by now."

"Hey!" Siena said. "In my defense, the signage was definitely not clear. And I *did* look at the map."

"Upside down," Meg added with a giggle.

"Okay, okay," Siena said. "So I'm a faulty navigator. Reading auras is way more interesting than reading road signs anyway."

She stared out the window, grinning. She didn't even have to set foot out of the car to know she loved this town. Its whole appearance seemed friendly and welcoming. Granted, she'd been in a good mood to begin with, so maybe that had something to do with it.

She'd ridden shotgun the whole way to Heidelberg, thanks to Chen and Meg, who had cleverly reasoned that they needed to sit side by side in the backseat to work on their math homework together. In the few hours' drive, the silent tension between her and Stefan evaporated, and by the time Heidelberg came into view, they were back on open, friendly, and even semiflirty terms. Siena had the whole weekend free of the Lebenhaus rules, and that meant anything could happen. She felt lighter and more in sync with her laid-back inner self.

This tiny university town seemed the perfect size for walking, its streets overflowing with outdoor cafés filled with students. Some seventy-degree weather had finally kicked into gear, and she was ready to do some exploring, and maybe even some partying, before she met Peter Schwalm tomorrow.

Stefan parked the car on the outskirts of town, explaining that most of the Aldstadt, or old town, was a pedestrian-only zone. They followed him through the rambling streets to their hostel. Siena immediately noticed a huge, multi-floor *Discotek* right around the corner.

"Check that out, ladies." She nodded toward the club. "The perfect locale. Two minutes from the hostel, and we can dance all night."

"Don't you need a good night's sleep before your big day tomorrow?" Meg asked.

"I can sleep in a future life," Siena said. She turned to Chen. "And there'll be no pining away for Ansel tonight, either."

Chen rolled her eyes. "I don't do pining. Besides, I just bought a new pair of boots that need debuting, so I might be convinced to go. Sans the dancing, of course."

"And what about you?" Siena threw Stefan a dare with her eyes. "Do you think you can keep up with us on the dance floor tonight?"

Stefan smiled but shook his head. "My friends and I have some catching up to do, so I have to say no." He

glanced at his watch. "I should get over to the dorm to meet them."

Stefan had decided to stay in the dorm with his buddies while the girls stayed in the hostel, but Siena wasn't ready for him to disappear just yet. The sweetness of spring was in the air, they were hours away from Dr. Goldstein (and Briana), and she had an inkling that the stars were on her side this time.

"Wait a sec," she said, stopping him. "Why don't you bring your friends along tonight? The university's just five minutes' walk from here, and we'll need you to protect us from any big, bad upperclassmen who find us irresistible." She leaned toward him, dropping the biggest, boldest hint she could. "We'll make a pact of secrecy. Whatever happens here stays between us."

Had she really just said that?

She chanced a sideways glance at Meg and Chen and saw Chen elbowing Meg to get her to close her gaping mouth. Yup, judging from Meg's reaction, she'd most definitely spoken the words. If anything was going to happen with Stefan, it was now or never.

She waited while he stared at the ground, seemingly weighing his options. Finally, he looked up at her with a mischievous grin. "Ten thirty tonight. We'll see you there." And with that, he turned and walked away.

• • •

Siena wasn't the only one who seemed to be infected with spring fever. She, Meg, and Chen found a tasty little eatery and enjoyed a few hours of boy watching and gabbing at one of the outdoor tables. Even Meg, who usually kept quiet about any boy but Cody, rated a few of the guys who passed. Siena finally managed to get a few details out of Chen about her most recent date with Ansel, and they all busted out laughing when Chen recounted that her first experience kissing a guy with facial hair was like "being smothered by a broom, but in a good way." But when it came time to get dressed for going out, Meg gave them the real treat for the evening. As Siena laid her clothing options on her bunk, Meg pounced on a mini with funky pink tassels lining the hem.

"Oooh, I love that," she said.

"You want to give it a try?" Siena asked cautiously, remembering how unsure Meg had been the last time she'd been faced with experimental dressing. But to her surprise, Meg nodded. She slipped it on, and Siena gave her a pink top to try with it. Meg spun around, letting the tassels fly out around her.

"Your legs look fab!" Siena cried, clapping.

Meg laughed, checking herself out in the wall mirror. "Can I borrow it for tonight?"

Siena couldn't believe Meg was *finally* going to wear a miniskirt. And with legs like hers, it was about time.

"More power to you, girlfriend," Siena said, then pointed to Chen, who was lying on her bed in full club garb, totally absorbed in composing. "Let's go, ladies! We have miles of dancing to go before we sleep."

Siena couldn't have picked a better dance club. It was five floors total, and every floor had a separate dance floor with its own DJ and music. She found Stefan and his university friends in the Blue Shark, the smaller club downstairs, with a darker techno vibe. Stefan had already grabbed a booth, and everyone made introductions. Adrian and Lucas, Stefan's friends, were so easygoing, even Meg seemed quick to relax. After sipping on her drink for approximately two minutes, Siena was already moving to the beat, even in her seat.

"All right." She stood up. "Who's going to break in the dance floor with me?"

"You know my answer to that one," Chen said, shaking her head, and then turned back to Lucas, the resident med student. "So what exactly is your theory on the chance of a future smallpox outbreak?"

Well, those two were down for the count, but Siena wasn't about to give up.

"Come on," she entreated, looking pointedly at Meg. But Meg wasn't quite ready to make the leap yet, either.

She had just resigned herself to hitting the floor by herself when Stefan stood up.

"Allow me," he said.

They started out on the dance floor with several feet of safety between them, but as the music heated up, dancers crowded the floor, and soon the two of them were so close Siena could smell his aftershave. His hands slipped lightly around her waist, at first only for a few seconds at a time, and then, finally, resting on her hips as they danced in sync with each other

As the night went on, Siena knew that something was different. Stefan hadn't danced with anyone else but her, and he'd even taken her hand a few times at their booth when they took breaks from the dance floor. She checked on Meg and Chen to make sure they were still having fun, but Meg seemed to be having the time of her life dancing with Adrian, who turned out to be the epitome of the non-threatening, big-brother type—perfect for her night out without Cody. And Chen and Lucas had been debating the pros and cons of stem-cell research, completely absorbed in a parallel brainiac universe. So it seemed that she and Stefan were being left alone, and she couldn't complain about that one bit. Stefan wasn't complaining, either. Every time their fingers touched, it was like an electric spark ignited between them.

They collapsed into the booth following Meg and Adrian's lead, laughing and out of breath.

"Could it be any hotter out there?" Siena said, taking a sip of her drink.

"You've been out there for almost an hour," Chen said. "Maybe that has something to do with it?"

"It is hot," Stefan said. But Siena noticed that he didn't take his hand from her waist.

"You two seem to be having a great time," Lucas said, smiling at them.

"That DJ's awesome," Siena said, dabbing her brow.

Stefan smiled, and suddenly reached over and pulled a damp strand of her hair off her forehead and tucked it behind her ear. The gesture sent shivers through her.

"Well, you look great on the dance floor," Lucas said. "A very cute couple."

Siena blushed and turned to hide her grin, but then she saw Stefan catch Lucas's eye and shake his head ever so slightly.

"We're not dating," he said quickly. And with that, his hand slipped from around her.

"Of course not," Siena added with a laugh, trying for a nonchalant recovery. But the whole table had fallen into an awkward silence, and Meg looked over at her with sympathetic eyes. This was the last straw.

She stood up, nearly dumping her water over on the table, but catching it just in time.

"You know, it's really stuffy in here," she said. "I'm going to get some air."

She pushed her way past crowds of dancers to the outside, vaguely hearing Meg calling after her somewhere in the background. But she couldn't stop. She wanted to keep going until she was as far away from the club, and Stefan, as possible.

Outside, the air was still a little warm, and the night was crystal clear. She crossed the Alte Brücke, the old stone bridge that spanned the river, and climbed onto the Philosophenweg. Stefan had mentioned earlier that this was the old Philosopher's Walk, where professors and philosophers from years gone by wandered and pondered all of their deep thoughts. Even as Siena rushed up through the narrow nature trail, she could smell the sweetness of the budding flowers surrounding her in the darkness. She finally sat down on a bench to catch her breath, and was awestruck by the city and castle in the distance, bathed in yellowish lamp glow. She didn't even hear footsteps approaching until they were only a few yards away.

"What was that all about?" Stefan said as he came up behind her.

She couldn't make out his expression in the darkness, but his voice held notes of worry. He sat down next to her just as fireworks exploded high over Heidelberg Schloss, sprinkling color across the sky.

"They shoot them off from Heidelberg Castle a few times a month," Stefan said, waving his hand at the sparkling display. "We came on the right night." He looked at her, waiting for her to say something.

Siena took a deep breath and then blurted out, "I don't

understand. I can't take this not-knowing-where-I-stand-with-you thing. Maybe I'm just imagining it. But I mean, one minute you're looking at me like you want to—" She stopped, feeling her face flush.

He leaned closer to her. "What?"

"I don't know," she mumbled, and sighed in frustration. Why was it that whenever she was around him, it seemed like the universe was conspiring against her for maximum humiliation? Fine. What the hell. Seize the humiliation. She pushed back her hair and threw up her hands. "Like you want to kiss me! Yes, and then the next minute you're back in RA mode. I know you have your job to worry about, but sometimes you seem to forget about it, and other times it seems like the most important thing." She didn't mention Briana because she figured if he really did have feelings for her, she'd know soon enough, without having to be snarky about it. "I just wish I could figure out what it is you want, one way or the other. I mean, what *would* happen if we kissed?"

She cursed herself for her verbal diarrhea. Now she'd screwed up everything. She wouldn't even be able to be friends with him after this. It would be too awkward.

She stood up to walk away, but Stefan grabbed her arm to stop her. He cupped her chin in his hands, lifting her face to his.

"Let's answer that question right now," he whispered, and kissed her.

She leaned in to him, but then pulled away. "Don't do that unless you want to."

"I've wanted to since I first met you," he said, running his hand through her hair. "I'm sorry I didn't do it sooner, but with my job, I knew I couldn't. It pays for my *Studiengebürhen*."

"I'm not even going to try to figure out what that means," Siena said with a laugh.

"Er, money for classes," Stefan said.

Siena nodded. "So what's different now?" she asked. "You'll still have your job to think about when we get back to Munich."

Stefan kissed her again. "Some things are worth taking a chance for."

As the fireworks lit up the night sky around them, she lost the will to argue, and let herself get lost in his kisses instead.

She was up before sunrise on Saturday morning. Today was the day that she'd been waiting for for so long, and she couldn't believe it was actually here. She dressed quietly, trying not to wake Meg and Chen. They'd met up with her and Stefan in the early A.M. as they made their way back to the hostel, and of course, after seeing the two of them with their arms wrapped around each other, had to have the whole story ASAP once Stefan left. All in all, she'd slept only a couple of hours, and she didn't want Meg and

Chen to lose out on their z's just because she was restless.

As she left the hostel to go find some breakfast, she smiled at her surroundings. The early-morning sun was just burning off the fog that had settled in the valley overnight, and the bright green hills and flowers shone with dew.

As she turned to make her way into the Old Town, she suddenly saw Stefan farther down the street, snapping photos of Brückentor, the gate to the Alte Brücke. Last night's kiss came back to her in a flash, and she suddenly had a mild freak-out session, wondering if today was going to be all weirdness with him now. Stefan looked up from his camera and smiled at her.

"Good morning," he said. "You couldn't sleep, either?"

Siena shook her head. "Too nervous."

"What's to be nervous about?" Stefan grinned. "I know I'm good-looking, but that shouldn't scare you."

"No." Siena laughed, lightly slapping his arm. "I'm nervous about meeting Peter. That's all."

"He'll be happy to see you."

"I know," Siena said. "But I'm not even sure what to say to him."

"Just talk to him about yourself, your family," Stefan said. "You're very charming, you know."

"Oh, is that right?" she teased. "You didn't seem charmed by me all the times you blew me off."

"That's not fair," Stefan said, pretending to be hurt. "I

did not have a choice. I was just trying to do my job the right way."

"And now?" she asked, her heart quickening.

"Now," Stefan said, packing up his camera, "I'm trying not to lose it." He grinned. "Come with me. I want to show you something."

He took her hand, and they walked through Heidelberg and up the hill leading to the Heidelberg Schloss. Fog and sunlight swirled around the castle ruins, giving the whole place a magical feel. There were no fancy wood carvings here, no turrets, no murals—just half-standing columns and a roofless ballroom under the wide-open sky. But the castle was more mysterious and striking because of it.

"The first buildings on the grounds were built in the late 1300s by Prince Ruprecht the Third, the rest by the prince electors of the sixteenth and seventeenth centuries," Stefan told her as he snapped a few shots of the crumbling walls.

They made their way to the castle gardens, and Siena soaked in all of the colors and smells surrounding her.

"This is the Elizabethan Gate," Stefan said, stopping in front of a beautiful stone garden gate. "Prince Friedrich the Fifth built it for his Scottish wife, Elizabeth Stuart. They were very much in love. Elizabeth married him even though her own mother disapproved, and they had thirteen children together."

"If that's not love, I don't know what is." Siena laughed.

"This gate was supposedly built overnight as a surprise for her birthday," Stefan said. "You can still see some of the creatures that were carved into it. According to the story, Friedrich promised Elizabeth one kiss for every creature she could find."

Siena walked closer to the gate, admiring its reddish brown color and romantic carvings. Stefan wrapped his arms around her.

"What are you doing?" he asked quietly, resting his chin on the top of her head.

"Counting," she said, pointing to the tiny creatures hidden in the stonework. "I've found five so far."

Stefan smiled, pulled her close, and kissed her gently. "One...two..."

At some point, she wasn't sure exactly when, she lost count.

Chapter Twelve

Siena and Stefan drove out to Weinheim together that afternoon. The village was tucked away in a wooded valley next to a winding mountain stream. It was only a short distance to drive, but it took a while because the roads were hilly. Siena didn't mind the extra time with Stefan. When she'd gone back to the hostel from the Heidelberg Schloss to get ready for the drive, she used the hostel Internet café to drop Lizzie a one-liner e-mail saying: *I finally made out with the Eurohottie!* Lizzie quickly replied with *It's about time!* When Siena filled Meg and Chen in on her latest

make-out session with Stefan, they pretty much said the same thing.

"I knew it was going to happen this weekend," Meg said. "It's a good thing, too. I was ready to knock y'all upside the head."

"I would have liked to see that happen," Chen said, laughing at the ridiculous threat.

"So," Siena said, opening up her suitcase to pick an outfit just right for her meeting with Peter, "do you guys want to come along to Weinheim?"

"We don't want to be a third wheel," Meg said. "Or fourth. You can tell us all about it later."

"Yeah, you two lovebirds have fun," Chen said. "We know when we're not welcome. We're going to check out the student prison museum here." She leaned toward Siena and whispered out of Meg's earshot, "Meg wants to see where we'll all end up if Dr. Goldstein finds out about our little weekend excursion. She'll probably have nightmares for weeks." She went back to her normal talking voice. "Besides, there's some killer heels I saw in that boutique around the corner. And you know what they say: 'Sales and shoes wait for no woman.'"

Meg laughed, and Siena tried her best to follow suit, but she was staring at the clothes in her suitcase with growing panic. Normally, she could throw together an outfit in nanoseconds, but today was different.

"What's wrong?" Meg asked as Siena threw a rumpled top back onto the bed.

"Help!" she said. "I'm not feeling the red or the orange." She threw two more tops down.

"Since when do you have clothing crises, bohemian queen?" Meg joked, but then got serious when Siena didn't laugh. "Okay, what about your favorite tee?"

Siena held up her Buddha tee, imagining seeing it through Peter's eyes.

"It's not right," she said. "What if he thinks it's strange?"

Meg touched her on the shoulder. "Hang on a sec, hon," she said. "Peter was your grandpa's friend. It doesn't matter what you wear. He's going to love you no matter what."

"And you know I'd never let you leave here wearing a questionable outfit," Chen said. "Those are all great options." She pointed at Siena's pile of clothes.

Siena paused, giving herself a reality check. Since when did she care about what other people thought of how she dressed? She wasn't going to start faking who she was when now seemed the most important time for her to *be* herself.

"You're right," she told them, pulling on her favorite peasant blouse. If she was going to get to know Peter Schwalm, then he was going to get to know the real her, too.

• • •

As Stefan circled the outskirts of Weinheim, Siena tried to swallow her nervousness. They turned down a dirt road bordered with acres of mountainside vineyards. Siena could smell the blooming roses that bordered each row. It was beautiful, and so peaceful. Finally, Stefan stopped in front of a little farmhouse with outbuildings scattered around it in cheerful chaos.

"He lives here, at the winery?" Siena asked in surprise.

"According to these directions," Stefan said. "It's the perfect place for me to take a long walk." He grabbed his camera as Siena stepped out of the car with her camcorder bag.

As they walked up to the door, Siena admired the carefully groomed pots of bright flowers along the front walkway. One thing she knew about Peter already—he was a nature lover, just like she was.

"I'll check in later, but take all the time you need."

She nodded, too nervous to say anything.

Stefan smiled, giving her hand a reassuring squeeze. "Relax. Enjoy the moment. Get to know him like your father never got to."

It was just what she needed to hear to dry up every ounce of stupid uncertainty she'd had. The whole reason she was here came back to her with full force, and her fear washed away.

"Thanks," she said, giving Stefan a quick peck.

She took a deep breath and knocked on the door. A

quiet shuffling sounded from somewhere inside the house, and the door opened. An old, wrinkled man with thin white hair was before her, but he stood straight and proud, and his huge, beaming smile matched the one she was sure was on her own face at that moment, too. She barely even noticed Stefan's little wave as he stepped back toward the vineyard, seeing that she was okay. Because before she could even utter one word, Peter Schwalm had wrapped her in a big bear hug.

The tea Peter had set on the coffee table had grown cold. Neither one of them had taken a single sip. From the minute Siena had walked through the door, they'd been talking nonstop.

The house held only the bare minimum, but what decor there was obviously held deep meaning. Filling one side of the living room was a wall of pictures, some black-and-white, of Peter as a younger man with his arm around a lovely woman, posing with two small children. The children grew through the photos, until, finally, in full color, they smiled out as adults, with children of their own who looked close to her own age. Stefan had been right when he said every picture told a story. These pictures were Peter's life.

"My family," he said, motioning to the photos. "My dear Marie is gone now, but the children and grandchildren are a joy."

"Where do they live?" Siena asked.

"Berlin," Peter said. "They like the metropolitan life. The fast pace."

"Do you see them a lot?"

Peter nodded. "They visit here a few times a year. The country is a nice change for the grandchildren. But me? I am done with Berlin." He looked out the window at his vineyards. "I have no need for that big city anymore. Now it is being rebuilt. It's new and fresh. But I prefer my grapes and my flowers." He smiled. "I promised myself I would move to the country someday, and here I am."

"It's beautiful here," Siena said. "I understand why you like it. But isn't it hard to be so far away from your family?"

"Sometimes," he said. "But I will never go back to Berlin. I said good-bye to too many friends, including your grandfather George, because of the Wall."

She leaned forward. "Did you help others cross the border, too?"

Peter nodded. "Fifteen of my dearest friends. I even helped some escape through a tunnel that was dug from an old bakery in the west to some outhouses in the east." He paused, looking a little sad. "I helped them all leave. I knew I had to. But I miss them still."

"But you stayed in Germany," Siena said. "Why?"

"My children were so young, and soon it was too dangerous to try leaving," he said. "There were shootings, horrible violence. I had to stop helping others, too. I couldn't put my family at risk. But I still loved this country, despite everything. I belong here. I will die here."

"Could you tell me how you helped my father and grandparents escape?" she asked. "My mom has told me the story before, but I'd love to hear it from you."

"Of course," Peter said.

Siena pulled her camcorder out of her bag. "Would you mind if I record it? I never want to forget any of this."

She wanted to get this all on film—for her mother, for herself, and someday, maybe even for her own children. This was living history, and part of her heritage. Peter agreed, and Siena hit *record*.

Peter spoke with real, vivid emotion, like he was reliving it all with every word. As she listened, Siena felt like she was there with him, too, sitting in his car on that night back in 1963, waiting and wondering if the guards would question him or search his car.

"Marie had sewn a Soviet uniform for me to wear, hoping that the border guards would let me through without questions," Peter said. "They stopped me, though, and asked what my business was. It was three in the morning, after all. I have never, to this day, been so terrified. Here was your grandfather George, with Christine and little William hidden under the hood. I didn't know how long they could stay in there, with little air and no space. Their lives were in my hands."

"What did you tell the guards?" Siena asked, totally mesmerized.

"I explained that I had been on weekend leave, but I had just received last-minute orders from my captain. A matter of great urgency. Couldn't they see I was in a rush? I had to cross immediately, and they were already making me late." Peter shook his head, remembering. "The whole time I was forceful. Cross with them. I wanted them to fear me. And the whole time, I had to grip the steering wheel so tightly because my own body was shaking with fear." He held up his hands, and they were trembling. "Even now, my heart races when I remember."

"Did the guards search the car?" she asked.

"No." He laughed. "They saluted me! Out of respect, you understand. And then they waved me on my way!"

She couldn't believe it. This was the first time she'd ever realized how close her family had come to being caught. How different her dad's life would have been without America, her mom, or even her!

"Your grandfather George," Peter said quietly. "He was my best friend. It broke my heart to know I'd probably never see him again. And then no word ever came of what had happened to him." He smiled and patted Siena's hand. "But now I've met you. I'd given up thinking I'd ever find out what happened."

"I know he wanted to send news to you," she told him. "I met my dad's cousin Anna, and she told me how everyone tried to find you. But it was impossible with the Wall."

For a fleeting moment, she wondered if Peter had ever tried to look up Grandpa George in America. But then she checked herself. She didn't see a television, let alone a computer, anywhere in the tiny house, although she did notice a newspaper on the kitchen table. Without a computer, she never would have found Peter, so it would have been pretty impossible for him to track her family without one.

Peter stood up. "Come with me, please. I'd like to show you something."

She grabbed her camera and followed Peter around the back of the house to a worn wooden shed. Peter pushed open the creaking door and stepped inside. Light streamed in through two high windows down onto an old Volkswagen Beetle, riddled with rust.

"This"—he patted the hood of the car affectionately— "was the car I drove that night so long ago."

Even in the seriousness of the moment, Siena couldn't help smiling at the thought of her dad being transported to freedom in a VW Bug. Such a cute, clichéd flower-power car for such a huge task.

"I have a feeling my dad would've loved seeing this if he were alive," she said. "It's sort of fitting for our family." Peter gave her a questioning look, and Siena just grinned. "You have to meet my mother."

"I'd like that," he said. He opened the hood of the car and pointed inside. "This is where your family hid. We

modified the fuel tank to make it smaller so that they could fit here."

Siena peeked into a small compartment near the fuel tank. "But that space would barely even fit a single child!" she cried.

"It did," Peter said. "And two grown adults. For four long hours."

She shook her head and stared, zooming in with her video camera.

"I still remember your father that night," Peter said. "William was just a toddler. He wasn't frightened by anything. George and Christine were terrified, as was I. But when we showed little William his hiding place in the car, he just laughed. It was a game of hide-and-seek for him, a grand adventure."

"From what I know of my dad," Siena said, "that was kind of how he lived his whole life."

"Good for him, then," he said. "That's what we all hope for our children. A life of grand adventures."

In that moment, she suddenly understood why the Carpe Diem List had been important to her father...why he must have created it in the first place. He had never forgotten his parents' fight for freedom, or Peter's, and that had to be why it was so important to him to live his life to the fullest.

As she and Peter kept talking, she told him all about life

in California—her mom, Sweet Sara's, Lizzie and Foster. But she also had a new part of herself to talk about. She told him about her time in Germany so far, her new friends, her classes. She didn't even realize how enthusiastically she was gabbing away until Peter burst out with a deep belly laugh.

"You certainly seem to love it here," he said.

Siena paused, and then broke into a grin. "I do."

And just like that, the piece she'd felt was missing since she came here—the piece of herself that didn't seem to fit anywhere in this country—snapped into place.

The time flew during her visit. Soon, long shadows fell across the living room, and Peter started to look a little tired. There was a knock at the front door.

"I should go," Siena said reluctantly. "I'm sure that's my friend. He's been waiting for me for a while now."

"Ah, yes," he said. "The young man who has been wandering through my vineyards."

She suddenly worried that she'd offended Peter by having this stranger traipsing around in his fields. "I'm sorry, we should've asked—"

"Don't you worry." Peter smiled. "I'm glad he's enjoying the vineyards. That's what they're there for."

As she started to say good-bye, she realized that she had not even stumbled once during their whole conversation in

German. When she'd really needed it, her language skills had finally kicked into full gear.

Peter handed her two bottles of wine. "They're from my last harvest. One is for you to enjoy with that handsome gentleman waiting for you. The other is for you to share with your mother—please toast your dad and grandparents and think of me."

"I have something for you, too." Siena pulled out the photo that Anna had given her, the one of her dad and grandparents in front of the Statue of Liberty.

"I think my dad would have wanted you to have this," she told him. "This was the first picture taken of them in America." Her eyes settled on Peter's wall of pictures, and he followed her glance.

"I will make a special place for it there," he said. "In my heart, I hoped I would be able to add one like this someday." His eyes filled with tears. "Thank you," he whispered.

"No," Siena said, wiping her own eyes. "Thank you."

"I'd love to hear from you again. You must write to me. Your grandfather and I were such close friends. I hope you and I can be, too."

"We will be," she said. "I promise to write you as often as I can."

"And next time you're in Germany," Peter said, "come back to see me."

He hugged her, and all too soon, she was stepping out the door.

"So?" Stefan asked when he saw her.

Siena took a deep breath. She wasn't sure there were words to describe everything that had happened. So she smiled instead. Stefan nodded, seeming to understand that words just couldn't do the trick.

"You're happy," he said, slipping his arm around her. "I'm very glad for you."

"Me, too," she said.

As the car pulled away, she kept her eyes on the farm-house until it disappeared from sight.

This day was the whole reason why she'd decided to make this trip to Germany, but the whole semester had become much more for her. It hadn't just been about finding Peter, it had been about finding parts of herself she'd never known she had. She'd never realized before how much she missed not having her father in her life. She and her mom had always been a team. Now she thought that maybe she was meant to find Peter all along. In fact, maybe her dad, wherever he was, had made that wish for her, too. She hadn't had a grandfather, or a father, for years, but now was her chance to have someone like that in her life. As they wound their way back toward Heidelberg, she took out the Carpe Diem List and wrote in *4/15/2006* next to Peter's name.

Chapter Thirteen

As Stefan pulled the car up in front of the Lebenhaus on Sunday night, Siena waited to take her lead from him. Now that they were back in Munich, she had no idea how things would be between the two of them. Meg and Chen discreetly said their good nights and got out of the car to head inside, leaving them alone.

After her day with Peter, the rest of her weekend in Heidelberg had flown by. She and Stefan had had what could only be called a "proper" date on Saturday night, going out for a nice quiet dinner together. They'd talked nonstop about his plans for his future and Siena's lack of plans for hers. Being with him was easy and comfortable, and so much fun. She came away from that night thinking that if she'd been able to stay in Germany longer than just another few weeks, he could've maybe been the start of something resembling a real, honest-to-goodness boy-friend. But that was one whopping if—an if she knew would never turn into a reality.

On the drive to Munich, they'd held hands, taking the time to enjoy a last little while with each other before Stefan's job became all too real again. Now here they were, both reluctant to get out of the car, neither one quite ready to let go.

"Hey," Siena teased. "I'll still be able to check you out from across the room, right?"

Stefan gave her an unsure smile, and she could see he was having a hard time with whatever he was about to say. "You know that we can't be seen—" he started.

"I know," Siena said, trying to make it easier for him. "You can't lose your job. I'm leaving in a few weeks. You can't risk that for me."

"I could quit," Stefan suggested. "Then we could be together for the rest of your time here."

She had to admit, it was a tempting solution. She'd love to spend her last few weeks in the throes of a foreign fling. But what would happen when she left for home? She wasn't a believer in long-distance things—they were way too restrictive to suit her style. It would never work. Plus,

Stefan needed this job, and she didn't want to be the cause of his losing it, especially since she couldn't say for sure that they had any kind of real future.

"No," Siena finally told him. "You need your job to help pay for school. I won't let you quit when I'll be gone soon anyway."

He didn't look happy about it, but he still seemed to know it was for the best. "Even if I can't show it," Stefan said, "I'll be thinking of you."

He kissed her softly, and she knew it might be their last kiss before she left. It was going to be hard to have any time alone together without chancing getting caught.

After a few sweet minutes, she forced herself to pull away from him. She got out of the car quickly, but not before she caught Briana staring at them through the front window of the dorm. The look on Briana's face said one thing—she knew the truth, and she was out for a kill.

"Oh, crap," Siena said, turning back to Stefan. "We have a problem."

An hour later, Siena and Stefan were sitting with Meg and Chen among the crowded tables at the Hofbräuhaus, the most touristy beer hall in Munich. After the run-in with Briana, Siena knew they needed a plan of action, and the sooner the better. As swarming with sightseers as it was, the Hofbräuhaus was the best place to go to avoid being surrounded by students from the program.

"Are you sure Briana saw you two?" Chen asked.

"Positive," Siena said. "You should've seen her face. We're dead."

"Maybe she won't go to Dr. Goldstein," Meg said.

"Meg, the girl didn't get the guy, *and* she was one-upped by Siena." Chen sighed. "They're dead."

Stefan shrugged and gave Siena a halfhearted smile. She knew he was trying his best to make light of the whole thing, but she could see worry creasing his face, despite the smile. "Well," he said to her. "Maybe I won't need to quit after all. Briana may have helped give me a way out."

"You're not going to lose your job," Siena said firmly. "Just because she had the hots for you doesn't mean she gets to get even."

"She had the hots for me?" Stefan asked in genuine amazement. "I had no idea."

Chen rolled her eyes. "Men never do."

"Briana isn't my type anyway," Stefan said, smiling at Siena. "She's too much of a—how do you say it in English?—um…high-nuisance woman?"

"High-maintenance," Siena said, laughing. "But *nui-sance* definitely describes her, too."

"Even if Briana does tell, Dr. Goldstein might not believe her," Meg suggested.

"But Dr. Goldstein loves her," Siena said. "Briana has the best grades of any student in the program. Her papers read like they're straight from the History Channel."

"Too bad they're not," said Chen. "Then we could resort to blackmail."

Suddenly Briana's last history paper came back to Siena in a flash. "Wait!" she cried. "They are! I mean, not from the History Channel. Briana read her last paper in class, and something about it bugged me. I didn't know what until just now." She smiled triumphantly. "She copied the whole thing from a library book. I'd read the excerpt she used when I was doing research for *my* paper. And I caught her with photocopies of book pages."

Maybe she had something on Briana, after all.

Siena smiled at Stefan. "Don't worry. I know just how to deal with this."

Once they all got back to the dorm (after a quick stop at the library), Siena went straight to Briana's room.

When Briana answered the door, the first words out of her mouth were, "I know why you're here, and you can save your breath. The only reason I haven't told Dr. Goldstein about your little duo is because she wasn't in her office when I stopped by earlier. As soon as she gets back, it's a done deal."

Siena held up a photocopy of the pages that Briana had copied into her last paper. "Are you sure you don't want to talk?" Siena asked.

Briana's eyes widened, and for a split second her glare

shifted to surprise. But just as quickly, her cool demeanor returned.

"About?" she asked impatiently.

"We could start with a little plagiarism," Siena said. "You and I both know you've been copying pages from library books for your history papers."

"I don't know what you're talking about." Briana sniffed.

"That's okay, because I'd be willing to bet that Dr. Schultz and Dr. Goldstein will know exactly what I mean when I show them these copies," Siena said. She'd never been big on ratting out other people, but she was kind of enjoying this *CSI* moment. "It will all be easy enough to prove when your paper and this copy are side by side."

Briana crossed her arms moodily, but didn't challenge Siena's argument.

Siena smiled. "So, here's the deal. You don't tell Dr. Goldstein about what happened with me and Stefan, and I don't tell about your little cheating episode."

Brian scowled, but muttered, "Fine."

Siena motioned to the photocopies. "I'll just hang on to these for a while."

She turned away, and nearly laughed as Briana's door slammed and an audible curse word sounded from the other side. Well, at least Stefan didn't have to worry about that anymore. Of course, she was absolutely positive she and Stefan couldn't let anything else happen between

them. Briana had agreed to the deal easily enough, but she knew it wouldn't be wise to press her luck.

She wasn't a rules kind of girl, but sometimes, Siena knew now, breaking them just complicated things. And she'd already filled up her rule-breaking quota. As a true yoga goddess would say—it was all about balance. If it was meant to happen, the greater powers at work in the universe would make sure that it did...someday. She knew better than to question timing. Who knew? Maybe in their next lives...For now, she was just glad she had a few great days with Stefan—no regrets. If that was all it ever came to, that would be enough.

Two weeks before the end of the semester, Dr. Goldstein took everyone on the long-awaited trip to Berlin. After the overnight train ride from Munich, Siena woke to a shaft of bright light peeking through the curtains of the sleeper car's window, right onto her face. She sat up, immediately banged her head on the ceiling of the car, and fell back groaning.

"Do you have to inflict bodily injuries on yourself this early in the morning?" Chen muttered from the other side of the car. "Some of us are sleeping."

"Rise and shine!" Siena said as she pulled back the curtain and displayed, with a flourish, the outline of Berlin against the red-hued sunrise. "We've arrived."

Massive was the best word to describe this city. It spread out for miles and miles, with none of the quaintness of Munich. This was a metropolis, complete with skyscrapers, streets already packed with cars and pedestrians, and a frantic feeling of progress.

"It's bigger than Houston," Meg said. "I think I like the size of Munich better."

"It's one of the biggest cities in Europe," Chen said with a yawn as the train pulled into the Bahnhof Zoologischer Garten station.

"Now I understand why Peter wasn't so keen on this city," Siena said. "It doesn't look anywhere near as peaceful as his vineyards. But it is something we definitely need to see before we all leave Germany."

In the weeks prior to this trip, Siena had gotten the sense that everyone felt the end of the semester coming all too soon. She'd even convinced Meg and Chen to take the "feng shui" tour of Munich, something she'd vowed to do before she left. They were all getting term papers ready and studying for finals, but that didn't seem as big of a deal as spending more time together. Sure, she still didn't have any idea what she was going to put together for her experimental film project, but she was hoping she'd find inspiration in this trip.

She had decided not to tell her mom anything about what had happened with Peter Schwalm until she got

home. Lizzie and Foster knew that she'd finally found him, but this was something she needed to talk about with her mom face-to-face. Her mom would understand everything, she was sure, and soon enough she'd be sharing the whole story with her.

With Stefan, she had become an expert at pretending like nothing had ever happened between them. It was doable, even though it had been a little tough at first. But at least she got to see him every day, and they still enjoyed talking and hanging out, just not alone. Every once in a while, though, she'd catch him sneaking her a secret smile meant for her eyes only, and sometimes she'd do the same for him. It was a little tiny way of showing each other that they both remembered.

Now Siena jumped off her bunk and peeked out into the hallway of the sleeper car. "Here comes Dr. Goldstein, doing her head count. We better get moving. It's time to *Bock auf* Berlin."

It was an expression she'd heard Stefan say when they were in Heidelberg, and he'd explained to her that it meant "go for it." She liked everything about the saying, so she'd quickly adopted it as a little mantra for her final weeks in Germany. She wanted to leave Germany knowing that, up to the very last minute, she'd sapped this country of every single thing it had to offer. She already had a *Bock auf* plan for her first day in Berlin. She'd been thinking this over since they'd boarded the train in Munich last night, but she was waiting to share it with Meg and Chen until they got settled in at the hostel.

The girls met up with the rest of the program on the train platform, and Dr. Goldstein led them all onto the U-Bahn. After a short ride, they arrived at their youth hostel, Gaeste-Spielzimmer. It was an old machine factory converted into a hostel, and Dr. Goldstein had booked the entire building for the long weekend.

The hostel management had a breakfast prepared, and after dumping her bags in their bedroom, Siena quickly filled a bowl with yogurt and muesli and a plate with cheese and cold meat and sat down to eat.

"What's your rush?" Chen asked, nodding at Siena's breakfast, which was half-gone within minutes.

"Okay," Siena said, ready to share her plan for the day. "I know Dr. Goldstein's taking us to the Wall this afternoon as a group, but I can't wait. We have free time until lunch." She pulled out her Berlin pocket guide. "I want to go now. I mapped out a walk we could take and everything."

Meg looked at her watch. "Siena, it's seven A.M. Everyone else is going back to bed for a few hours. Chrissy and Mia even skipped out on breakfast to sleep. It's not such a bad idea."

"I know, but this is something I need to do on my own, before we do it with the pack later on. I want as much time there as I can get. And it would mean a lot to me if you guys were there with me."

She didn't want to get shuffled around in a tour group this afternoon without first exploring the Wall the way she'd wanted to ever since she'd heard her dad's story. After meeting Peter, doing this on her own terms was even more important to her.

Meg and Chen agreed to go, and as soon as they all finished breakfast, they took the train to Potsdamer Platz. According to Siena's map, they would be able to walk from there to different spots of interest along the Wall. They emerged from the Potsdam underground station into a congested downtown center surrounded by skyscrapers.

"This is all new construction," Chen said. "A lot of the older buildings were destroyed during border installations when the Wall went up."

Just looking around her, Siena could see how much Berlin was still being rebuilt. Construction cranes dotted the skyline everywhere. It was exciting to be standing in the middle of it all, but she understood why Peter wouldn't want to live in this chaos.

They walked to the Brandenburg Gate, Berlin's only city gate, which had been closed for almost thirty years when the Wall was standing. The proud columns of the gate stood out against the morning sky, opening up to the rest of the world beyond the city.

Checkpoint Charlie, a short distance from the gate, wasn't much to look at, but it was still a powerful reminder of the old border controls between the east and west. It had been the crossing point where Western military forces and foreign tourists had to be checked out before entering East Berlin. The Checkpoint Charlie Museum gave lots of history about the Wall and the violent protests and arrests that had taken place during the Cold War. After walking through the museum, they headed toward the Wall Memorial and the Bernauer Strasse.

"The Wall ran right in front of people's houses here," Siena said in wonder.

"I don't see how people could stand living like that," Meg said quietly.

Siena stopped at a small plaque on the corner of Strelitzer Strasse, commemorating "Tunnel 57," the tunnel that had run between Bernauer Strasse and Strelitzer Strasse.

"I can't believe it!" she cried. "Peter helped coordinate the escapes through this tunnel." She hurriedly pulled out her camcorder and zoomed in on the plaque. "Fifty-seven people made it to freedom," she said. "That's amazing. And to think that man is living on a tiny farm in Weinheim."

"I think Abe Lincoln said something like 'Common-looking people are the best in the world,'" Chen said.

Meg smiled. "That makes perfect sense. The little heroes go unnoticed but make the most difference."

Between Ackerstrasse and Bergstrasse, they saw the

"death strip," where the remains of the old electrically charged border fence still stood. Beyond it was the grassy, deserted area where over a hundred and seventy people trying to escape had been killed. Here, Siena learned from her guidebook, border guards had orders to shoot to kill, and that's just what they did.

From that sobering image of the Wall, she led the way to the East Side Gallery, where the longest strip of the Wall was left, still standing, for visitors to take in. Unlike the death strip, panels of the Wall here were painted vibrant colors, all by different artists, to commemorate and honor, protest against communism, or celebrate freedom. There was a mix of joy and heartache all rolled into one here.

She stared at the Wall, seeing so clearly how it must've looked when her dad and grandparents had escaped all those years ago. It looked so small to her now, but it had been a prison for so many people.

She caught a glimpse of a little boy, about three or four years old, standing in front of the old piece of wall, and she grabbed her camcorder to get him on film. The boy was just about the age her dad had been when he had escaped. Siena hit *record*, zooming in on the blond-haired boy as he looked up at the wall.

Suddenly he gave the wall a good, swift kick, surprisingly hard for a boy so small. She had no idea what had prompted that, probably just a little boy fooling around, but she instantly felt the urge to do the same exact thing. Instead, she just smiled from behind the camcorder and kept filming until the boy took his mother's hand and disappeared into the crowd.

Someone tapped her on the shoulder, and she finally looked up.

"Siena," Meg said. "It's after noon. We should get back to the hostel."

She nodded, and reluctantly followed Meg and Chen to the U-Bahn. Meg and Chen talked the whole ride back, but Siena stayed quiet, lost in her thoughts. Meg looked over at her once, but seemed to understand her silence without questioning her, and just gave her a small smile instead.

She'd seen so much in Germany—the beauty of the countryside, the friendliness of the people, the tragedy and glory of much of its history. Everything here had started out as such a mystery to her, but now she understood more of where her dad came from, and how she tied into it all. She'd found her place, and for the first time, the country of her ancestors felt like her second home.

She watched the film clips she'd taken that morning through the viewfinder on her camcorder, the images of the Wall, and the face of the little boy as he stood before it. In that instant, she knew what her film for the German experience would be about...capturing every last detail of

the complex jumble of emotions she felt about this country.

For the rest of the weekend, she toured with the program, visiting the Gemaldegalerie of art, the Reichstag building, and Bellevue Palace. Time flew, and she enjoyed seeing it all. Still, all she could think about was getting back to Munich to put together her film.

Chapter Fourteen

To: sagittarigurl@email.com
From: yogamama@email.com
Subject: Tofu Turn-off

My tofu burgers just don't taste the same without you, chickadee. So don't get any ideas about running off to Morocco with Stefan. At least not until you're eighteen. Even if he is as cute as he sounds, *and* he's a photographer. I'm holding off on making the usual shopping trip to "Everything Under the Sun" until you get back. You're the

one with the thrift store knack anyway. See you soon!

Love,

Mom

On the last day of class, Siena waited anxiously for Dr. Nielson to hand back the experimental film projects. Her finals had all gone pretty smoothly, thanks to the diligent studying she'd done, and the drilling from Chen worthy of the best military sergeant. She'd gotten an A-plus on her final history paper, head-to-head with Briana, who had gotten her A by much less worthy means. And to her surprise, and Chen's, she'd aced her German final, a true testament to how in tune with her ancestors' country she'd really become.

Her film, though, had taken the most prep time. She had worked for hours in the lab putting it together—editing, splicing, adding in some special cinematic effects. Ansel had even shown her how to dub in some background music.

She was proud of how it had turned out, but she was still eager to see what Dr. Nielson thought of it. She took a deep breath as he slowly made his way up and down the aisles, returning the DVDs to the students. He got to Ansel's desk and clapped him on the shoulder.

"Excellent work," he told him, and Ansel, shocker, actually broke into a full-toothed grin, something Siena never thought she'd see.

She waited for Dr. Nielson to come to her, but he never did. While everyone whispered about their grades, her heart sank. So he'd hated it, then. He was just waiting until after class to tell her privately. Well, if she got a C in this one class, it wouldn't kill her. Just then, Dr. Nielson announced that there was one film he wanted to share with the rest of the class.

"This film is truly unique," he said. "It portrays the living history of this dynamic country. It exemplifies the struggles the German people have encountered throughout the years, and the courage human beings have to live fully and freely."

He dimmed the classroom lights, and an image of the Brandenburg Gate filled the screen. Siena clutched her desk, leaning forward. This was *her* film! Peter Schwalm's voice came over the speakers as images flashed across the screen. There was the crematorium at Dachau, the little boy craning his neck up at the Berlin Wall, and finally, a shot of the peaceful vineyards of Peter's winery blending in with the flowers.

"I knew," Peter's voice was saying, "that I had to help my friends, my countrymen, to get to freedom. As Goethe once said, 'To think is easy. To act is hard. But the hardest thing in the world is to act in accordance with your thinking.' I knew I had to act. I could not have lived with myself otherwise."

When it was projected on that huge screen, the film

seemed much more dramatic. Siena tried to make out people's reactions in the darkness. From what she could see, everyone was staring at the images with utter seriousness. The film ended, and for every second of silence in the room, she held her breath. Then the entire class erupted into applause, and she finally gave a relieved smile.

Ansel whispered to her cryptically, "Your blood, your brilliance."

"Um, thanks?" She *thought* that was some sort of artsy compliment.

As the students left class, Dr. Nielson came over with her DVD in hand.

"Excellent work," he said. "Would it be all right if I made a copy of this? I'd like to show it to my students next semester. It's the perfect example of the heartfelt films I want from them."

"Sure," Siena said. She stayed while he made a copy, then she left the campus for the last time, wearing a huge grin. She walked past the student café, the clock tower, the research library. She'd accomplished everything she came here to do, but she'd gained more than she ever thought she would.

That Saturday, the entire program made the short trip from Munich to the *Frühlingsfest*, or Spring Festival, at Theresienwiese for a May Day celebration. Now that finals were over with, Siena was ready to let her free spirit self take complete control again.

She wasn't the only one ready for fun. Everyone on the train was rowdy, relaxed, and laughing. Stefan and the other RAs seemed less like they were on the job and more like they were kicking back as best buds. Dr. Goldstein, usually dressed primly in blazers or suits, was wearing jeans and joking around with the students. Even Briana's catty clique didn't annoy Siena like it normally did.

"This is my kind of holiday!" she cried as they deboarded the train and she looked at the huge *Frühlingsfest* field, with its countless beer tents, carnival rides, food booths, and games. "The flowers are blooming, the grass is green-ing, and here we will embrace spring in all its pagan glory."

"You're not going to strip and dance around a fire pit or anything, are you?" Chen said. "Because somehow I don't think we'll be able to convince the police that you're per-forming rites of spring."

Siena just laughed at Chen, who had brought Ansel and some of his buddies along for the day, too. "You've got a little spring fever yourself. Admit it." She whispered so only her friend could hear, "Since when have you ever held hands with Ansel in public before?"

Chen shrugged and blushed. "I'm willing to let my aver-sion to PDA go for one day."

"I think we should make our first stop there," Meg said

with a rebellious but shy smile, pointing to a beer tent.

Siena grinned and grabbed her hand. "Quick, let's go before you change your mind!"

After a short stop at the beer tent, they filled up on some bratwurst and kraut in the outdoor eating area. Just as they were getting up, there was an announcement over a loudspeaker for the May queen contest.

"May queen?" Siena asked.

"The queen who heralds the arrival of spring," Ansel explained. "There's a dance contest. The dance is called a *Schuhplattler*, one of the traditional folk dances in Bavaria. Men jump, stomp, and slap their feet with their hands while woman spin around them."

"It sounds like some horrific German form of square dancing," Chen said.

"It is," Ansel said. "In this contest, women from the audience are paired up with professional folk dancers. You'd be surprised how hard it is to keep spinning like that. A lot of girls can't do it for long. The girl who outlasts the rest with her folk dancing partner is crowned the May queen."

Siena jumped up from the table. Sure, it sounded a little cheesy, but she had to at least give it a try while she was here, in honor of all her German ancestors before her. "It's my true calling!" she said. "Show me the way."

Ansel and Chen rolled their eyes in unison, confirming their complete soul-mate status. Ansel led Siena and their friends to the dance contest, set in a wide-open field of fresh green grass.

She went out to stand in the field with the other girls joining in the contest, and saw Briana doing the same. The male folk dancers politely paired up with each of them. Siena's partner was a sweet-looking bearded man name Hans.

"You just keep spinning, yes?" he said. "I do the rest of the work."

Siena nodded and grinned.

"Go Siena!" Meg yelled from the crowd, and Siena curtsied in her direction just as the music started. There was one costumed woman in the middle of the field who was obviously trained, and she led the way, showing the rest of the girls the proper steps. Siena watched the woman's movements, and when she thought she had the steps down, she began. Hans was dancing around her, alternately jumping into the air and slapping his knees and feet with amazing speed. At first, it was hard for Siena not to get dizzy, but then she found if she kept her eyes focused on something, it was easier. Other girls started to drop out slowly, fumbling the steps. But Siena kept going, holding her head up high. All of her happiness burst out in her clapping hands and stomping feet.

She was having such a great time she had no idea how much time passed before Hans held out his hands to stop her. It was only then that she looked around to see that

she'd outdanced every other girl in the running, including Briana (tee-hee). A woman in medieval costume approached her with a wreath bursting with colorful flowers.

"This year's May queen," she said to the crowd, placing the wreath on Siena's head. "Winter has now officially been defeated."

Meg and Chen hooted and clapped, and there was a loud whistle from the crowd behind her, which, she discovered when she turned, had come from a beaming Stefan. She couldn't stop smiling, thinking that this was the perfect Carpe Diem moment.

Afterward, the maypole-climbing contest was announced, and she, as queen, was asked to oversee it.

"It's your job to bestow a kiss to the victory climber," the contest coordinator explained.

"My pleasure," she said, hoping that there would be some real cuties putting their biceps to work. At the climbing area, ten tall tree trunks were lined up, each shining with grease to make them as slippery as possible. At the top of each pole was a bundle of pretzels and sausages for the victor. She happily noted a couple of very cute guys getting ready to climb.

"Siena," Chen hissed, elbowing her.

"Ouch! What?" Her eyes followed to where Chen was pointing, and there was Stefan, stepping up to one of the greased maypoles. Her heart flip-flopped like mad. This certainly made things interesting.

A bell sounded, and all ten men leaped up onto their trees. The newbies slid their way down the poles almost immediately. A few more made it halfway up before struggling and then slipping to the ground.

Her heart really went wild as she watched Stefan climb his way steadily upward, faltering only once. At the top, he pulled the pretzels and sausages from the pole and then slid down, triumphantly holding his prizes.

"If the May queen would please bestow a victory kiss to the winner," the announcer said.

Stefan climbed up onto the stage where Siena was already standing. She felt the heat rise in her cheeks. Everyone from the program, including Chrissy, Mia, Briana, and even Dr. Goldstein, was in the crowd watching.

"Kiss him!" everyone was yelling, and Dr. Goldstein was no exception.

Stefan was so close to her she could touch him, a huge, mischievous grin on his face. The rules didn't seem to apply under these circumstances—much to her delight, and his, too, it seemed.

"Well?" she said. "Who are we to go against tradition? Should we give the crowd what they want?"

Stefan's smile widened. "Absolutely."

The kiss was short and sweet, but she whispered before Stefan pulled away, "You won on purpose, didn't you?"

Stefan laughed. "I wasn't about to let anyone else have that kiss."

They waved before leaving the stage, and Siena caught a glimpse of Briana frowning in the back of the crowd. She couldn't help feeling just the tiniest bit smug. After all, rules could be bent when the forces of the cosmos were at work, and those were the times she lived for.

As the sun set, everyone in the program piled into one of the food tents for their last dinner together before flights home the next morning. The tent was lined with booth after booth of all sorts of different German foods. Siena, Chen, and Meg all decided to get something different to eat so that everyone could share bites. They grabbed a table together and spent the whole meal laughing and talking, tired after the full day at the fair but wanting to spend as much time with one another as possible. Chrissy and Mia sat near them, too, and soon they'd all started a small competition to see who would be willing to try the oddest food choice. Siena won hands down when she tried Hamburger Aalsuppe, eel soup. That had to be right up there with some of her dad's exotic food choices.

As plates started to empty, Dr. Goldstein stood to give a toast.

"For a wonderful, memorable semester of joy, learning, and friendship, I thank each and every one of you!" she said, raising her glass.

At that, Stefan began handing out mini-photo albums

to each of the students to remember their semester. He gave everyone hugs, too. When he came to Siena, he pulled a photo album from the very bottom of the pile.

As he hugged her he whispered, "You know if I could've, we would have had more."

"I know," she said, giving him a smile to let him know that it was all okay.

Even though she wished they could have had a few minutes alone to say a better good-bye, she knew she'd have to be happy with this. Just hearing him say that was enough for her.

Back in their room later that night, Siena and Meg slowly took down their feng shui decor.

"You keep the colored beads," Siena said, handing them to Meg. "You'll need them to balance out your mom's decorating at home."

Meg laughed. "That's for sure," she said.

Siena packed a beer stein for Foster and some lederhosen, too (she couldn't resist), a great European top for Lizzie, and some authentic German Kaffee for her mom. As she zipped her bags shut and looked around at the now bare walls of their dorm room, it really hit her that the semester was over.

Just then, Chen stuck her head around their door. "In the mood for some company?" she asked.

"Did Ansel leave?" Siena asked. He'd come over after their dinner to say good-bye to Chen.

Chen nodded. "I don't even feel like poetry tonight. I can't believe it. What if I'm blocked forever because of a guy?"

"You won't be," Siena said. "Hey, heartache can sometimes make masterpieces. Just give yourself a little time."

"He said he could maybe come visit me in Boston next Christmas," she said. "He's never been to the States before."

"That's great!" Meg said. "Christmas'll be here before you know it."

Chen nodded.

"And you'll have us to e-mail in the meantime, too," Siena said. "There's the Old Spanish Days Fiesta in Santa Barbara every summer. Maybe you guys could come out for that."

"Or y'all can come see me in Texas!" Meg said. "Chen, you can see firsthand how sausage is really made."

"No thanks," Chen said. "Sometimes ignorance really is bliss."

Chen reached into a shopping bag she'd brought in with her. She pulled out a book titled *Siddhartha* and gave it to Siena. "It's by Hermann Hesse. He's a great German writer," she told her. "It's about Buddha as a teenager."

"Thanks!" Siena said, giving Chen a big hug. "I have something for you, too," she said, handing Chen a blank leather-bound book. "It's time you broke away from text-book poetry. This is a way better channel for those muses."

For Meg, Chen had a pair of killer knockoff Prada shoes and Siena had a pink-sequined halter.

"For your dancing diva self," Siena told her, having conspired with Chen on the outfit earlier.

Meg gave Chen a book of Heinrich Heine poetry and Siena one of her country music CDs. "I caught you singing along with this one," she said to her. "Admit it."

"Never," Siena said with a smile, but she was already tempted to start humming one of the songs.

They all exchanged long hugs, phone numbers, and addresses.

"So," Siena said as they finally collapsed on the beds, bags all packed and ready, "I still haven't tried out my henna tattoo kit. It's now or never."

Meg took a little convincing, but finally, she and Chen each picked out a design.

Meg chose a pretty pattern for her hands that symbolized courage, something she said she wasn't even sure she'd had before this trip. Chen picked one for her ankle symbolizing love crossing great distances.

"Does this have anything to do with a certain cine-martist I know?" Siena teased.

She set to work painting the patterns and was pleased when they came out beautifully. For herself, she painted the symbol of family wrapping around her wrists and up

her forearm—family lost and found, old and new, loved and never to be forgotten.

The girls stayed up all night talking and, as the sun came up, made their way downstairs to the bus.

"No tears," Chen said as they finally reached their separate security gates at the airport. *"Alles hat ein Ende, nur die Wurst hat zwei."*

Siena translated in her head and then exclaimed, "Everything has an end. Only the sausage has two?" She laughed. "Totally random, but true."

"I'll do anything to prevent crying," Chen said with a warm smile.

Siena nodded, while next to her, Meg just sniffled and wiped her eyes.

They all shared one more hug, none of them wanting to be the first one to turn away. Chen finally went first, then Meg (after another five minutes of tears), and last Siena, looking after both of her friends as they disappeared through the gates.

As her plane took off, she tried not to cry. She'd held it in while she'd said her good-byes, but as all the great memories of the semester rushed back to her, her eyes filled. She pulled out the photo album Stefan had given her, thinking that maybe looking at the pictures would help cheer her up. When she opened the album, a picture slipped out into her lap.

It was a photo of Stefan, smiling for the camera. On the back of the photo, there was a note in his writing: *So that when you come back to Germany next time, you'll still recognize me. I hope it won't be too long from now.*

He'd written his e-mail and phone number down, too. She put his e-mail and phone number right into her organizer (Chen would be proud). While she was at it, she wrote in Anna's and Peter's addresses, too.

She smiled and wiped her eyes, reading over Stefan's note one more time before slipping it back into the album. She probably wouldn't make it back to Germany anytime soon, but who knew? Now that she had some surrogate family members here, not to mention a potential European hottie, she definitely had lots to come back for. She did want to start traveling a lot more, too. She'd done it once, and already she couldn't wait for next time. She could go anywhere and do anything.

She looked down at Munich through the plane window, watching the steeples get smaller and smaller, until finally the outline of the city was gone in the clouds. Then she reached into her backpack and pulled out a piece of paper. At the top she wrote: *Siena Bernstein's Carpe Diem List.* There were so many things she wanted to do, and now was the perfect time to start.